I0664880

Destiny

Destiny

By Andre "Dre" Cooper

Street Dreamz presents
Destiny

Self-Published with assistance from
MIDNIGHT EXPRESS BOOKS
POBox 69
Berryville AR 72616
MEBooks1@yahoo.com

Destiny

By Andre "Dre" Cooper

Chapter 1

Screeching tires could be heard as the four SUVs rounded the street, and sped down the back road of Ancon Hill, in a single file. The two-lane road had been empty this morning except for the occasional peasant-farmer strolling alongside the road with his flock of sheep or goats. But other than that, no trucks carrying goods to the surrounding boroughs, no tourists pulled on to the side taking pictures of the city, or travelers could be found on the road.

The black Suburbans, with presidential tints, nearly came to a complete halt, but rather slowed down. The third Suburban, in line, had suddenly caught a flat tire.

"What was that?" Luis asked from the backseat.

"I think we just caught a flat." Tito responded back then held his left hand close to his ear, in order to listen to the chatter going on.

The SUVs pulled to the side and parked on the small dirt road. Panama City's large belt of rainforest was in full view, as was the Gulf of Panama. The water shined and sparkled from the rays giving off by the sun beating down on the green water. Yachts, commercial boats, and smaller fishing boats could be seen traversing through the green waters. While the skyline remained dense, due to the tropical rainforest, the high-rises and other commercial buildings could be seen.

A crew of four men got out of the first Suburban. They were garbed in black business suits, dark sunglasses, and heavily armed. Small earpiece wires hung out of their ears, which were used to communicate with the other members on the detail. They headed back to view the third Suburban. The second vehicle filled with four members also got out of third SUV, and strolled with the others.

The driver of Tito's vehicle was also out along side Tito when the others stepped up.

"So, who's going to take care of this?" One of the men asked nobody in particular. He was just trying to lighten the tense mood.

"I'll take care of it. Just secure the perimeter and Marco radio command and inform them of our stop."

"Si Senor." He replied then went into his inside suit jacket then pulled out the phone.

After Tito relayed his order to the detail they went about, and appeared to be doing their job.

Tito was a native of the country, and head of the Matta's family security detail. The twelve men Tito had under his command today were just a small portion of his detail. The family had over forty others. Most were natives of Panama, and the others were new recruits from different American security firms who specialized in protecting American and foreign diplomats.

Three men, dressed in business suits and dark shades, leaped out of the last Suburban. The doors swung open simultaneously which caused the others to glance in their direction. The men rushed over to the group with their assault rifles raised high.

"Hands in the fucking air! In the fucking air!" One of the armed men yelled, in a crisp American accent.

Tito's men froze from the command and didn't bother to reach for their weapons.

The confusion and yelling caused Luis and his brother, Pedro to turn in their seats. They glanced out the back window of the Suburban. Two armed men had drawn down on the detail while the other armed men raced directly over to vehicle.

"What the hell?" Luis yelled. Pedro dove forward and landed in the driver seat head first. He maneuvered, quickly, and positioned himself in an upright angle.

Tito rose up, slowly, with his hands in the air. He glanced around at his men. They all seemed defeated and scared. He knew they didn't stand a chance against these well-trained men.

"Don't think about it, shit head!" The armed man said, to Tito. He seen the look on his face and knew it well.

Pedro frantically searched the ignition and surrounding area for the keys. They were gone. The driver had taken them out of the ignition upon departing the vehicle. Pedro tried the automatic start button. He pressed and-pressed hard. The engine wouldn't turn.

"Shit!" Pedro's fingerprint identification wasn't a match.

The door flung open on Pedro. He was snatched out of the SUV by his suit's collar then thrown on the dirt. The other armed man then raced to the backdoor and snatched it open. Where, he found Luis froze and in utter disbelief that this was actually happening to him. *A kidnapping!* No, not to anybody affiliated with the Matta family. Luis thought to himself, as the man pulled the door open.

The Matta's were powerful and influential in Panama. Their history stretched back to the days of the Noriega regime. Where, the Matta brothers had acted as money launders and, transporters of guns, drugs and ammunitions for the regime.

At the time, Luis and Pedro owned several trucking companies. With the business and help of Noriega, the brothers became multi-millionaires quickly around this era, which at that point, they started to branch out and invest in other lucrative opportunities in Panama. Like operating loan offices, importing and exporting fruits and vegetables and buying large plots of land around the Port of Balboa.

In or around 1989, when Noriega was kidnapped, indicted and

extradited to the United States, the Matta family had became a powerful clan. The Americans confiscated and froze all of Noriega's accounts. Seized his businesses, homes and the military from him.

The United States did not bother any of Noriega's associates or coconspirators in his illegal drug empire but placed one of their own in place. Guillermo Endara was shoved into power to run the affairs of Panama.This moved by the United States indicated to all interested parties that the cocaine business was still in full swing.

Luis scooted out of the vehicle without the help of the armed man. He did not bother to raise his hands as the others had done. "How much do y'all want? I am a wealthy man that will pay a lot for our freedom."

Kidnapping was a lucrative business in Panama, and nobody was exempt from it. That's why it was imperative to have reliable and well-trained men who were willing to die defending you. But, Luis had made an enormous error of judgment. He hired people outside of his country, Americans.

They didn't bother to entertain Luis's last statement. The armed man stepped back and fired. "Blac! Blac! Blac!" The two other armed assassins followed suit and sprayed the ten others like dogs. "Blac! Blac! Blac! Blac! Blac! Blac! Blac!" The machines loud blasts erupted and could be heard for miles above the scenic hills of Panama City.

The armed men stopped mowing down the group then ran up and fired upon Luis's team while they lay prostrated on the ground.

They were trying to make sure the job was done. No excuses could be made or giving to the organization that ordered this massacre.

The armed men completed the executions and hurried back to the Suburban. They leaped in the vehicle and sped off into the Hills of Ancon.

Chapter 2

The view of a pale blank of mist and clouds stormed through the two enormous, floor-to-ceiling, windows. The long burgundy drapes had been pushed to the side so it wouldn't obscure the view. This was an iconic scene. The view displayed an ancient type of atmosphere of foreign grandeur which accentuated the spacious room. Across from the window stood a huge oak cabinet with expensive china inside. A long oak table also decorated the center of the room with fifteen wooden chairs, with soft stuffed silk coverings, on each side and one at both ends.

Laptops sat, neatly, in front of each person seated around the table along with a folder, a glass cup, and a pitcher of water.

The gloomy day tried to sway the emotions and concerns brewing in the room but it couldn't. This was a historic event occurring in the back country of New York State. A meeting like none before or to be repeated in the near future.

Naseem Gordon sat at the head of the table. A large painting by Rembrandt hung on the wall behind Naseem. He also had a laptop, folders filled with documents and a water pitcher in front of him. Naseem studied the contents of the computer, intently. Just like the rest of the people. Occasionally, he glanced up to view the other people. He wanted to see if they were soaking the information in and buying into the vision he created for the immediate future.

The video came to an end. Naseem was the first to raise his head. "Now, after viewing the video I presented concerning the major distribution areas, key investors and the predicted net profits it shows a clear picture on how we, collectively, could bring this vision to a reality... Let's debunk this myth or stereotype that we can never organize and come together in order to make a change without violence and killing each other." He relayed the message with a confident tone.

Most of the crowd gave slight nods of approval. But, there were also those who faces showed some confusion and a few appeared hesitant.

Naseem had created a perfect outline and displayed how this particular group could gain control over the distribution aspect of the declining cocaine business. An aspect of the business that had always been controlled by outsiders-- foreigners, not Americans or African-Americans, as it should have been from the beginning. For the simple reason that, African-Americans were the ones most affected by the drug epidemic. Their homes were the ones who were getting torn apart. They were the ones being thrown in prison for decades at a time by being tricked by the foreigners to rat out each other. And, the last example Naseem set out was that the blacks were the only ones who could control the cities, and neighborhoods where the drugs were being sold. The Colombians, Dominicans and even the Mexicans couldn't or wouldn't be able to set up shop, in order to sell their drugs without the blacks help, support and muscle. He tried to hone in on these facts and sway them over to his ideal.

Naseem was adamant about this project, and wanted it to prosper. He knew the harsh realities that the drug business brought with it. Naseem grew up in the gritty streets of Chester, Pennsylvania and seen the old days when cocaine flourished as king and also seen how it destroyed the communities. By being African-American, as some or all blacks identified themselves, who were born and raised in the United States, they deserved better and should be compensated handsomely from the business.

He was smart enough to know that drugs weren't going anywhere. America had a problem and would remain the number one consumer of drugs, with the blacks at the top of this list, and that such people as the politicians, government agents and organizations closely tied to the interest groups were going to dictate this fact.

Naseem let his words sink in their minds before going on. "Now does anybody have any questions? Fill free to expound on any aspect of the plan because, as of now, it's just a tentative plan. We can make adjustments, as any of us sees fit... We're here to work as a group but with the structure of a Fortune 500 business. It's the only way I see us being able to pull this off and be successful."

The language Naseem spoke to the group wasn't lost on them. This was an exclusive group of people. They were the *crème de la crème* of America's drug trade. Pennsylvania, California, New York, Washington, Detroit, Texas, Baltimore, and Arizona were just some of the states and cities that were in attendance. Naseem knew some of these individuals from his college days, some from being out and about at a few of the upscale parties, shows, and the others were selectively picked by their stature in the drug business. There were close to 6-7 hundred million or more sitting around the table. These men and women were not only involved in selling drugs. They were also owners of lucrative businesses. Gas stations, truck companies, real estate, record labels and convenient stores just to name a few.

"Yes, I have a question." A petite woman named Crystal from Detroit says. She was dressed moderately in a black business skirt set with nude Jimmy Cho shoes on. Crystal had deep pockets, and was smart and articulate with a powerful alliance to the Gulf Cartel. "So my understanding of this whole meeting is that you want us to give up our supplier names, stop dealing with them, place our money in a central company or source and..."

"Exactly," Naseem replied then headed over towards the window His brown Ferragmo loafers didn't make a sound on the floor. The room was still and everybody stood there wondering. *Was this the right person to lead us? Was this all a hoax to get the money at a central account then dash off with it? Did he even understand the significance of such a request?* Naseem turned to face the group. He rolled up his white cotton dress shirt, above his wrists, showing a simple Chopard gold watch. Naseem then straightened out his denim jeans before speaking.

7

"We have the advantage over these people. Let's flex our muscles a little. How long have we been pawns in the Mexicans, Colombians and Dominicans games? We have to take what is rightfully ours... Then, we can dictate the prices, purity, and flow of the drugs. We'll dictate who makes money and who starves... Not them! Let's take a look at the current prices, and the purity now." "There forty plus on the retail level." Web from St. Louis said. The others nodded in agreement.

"Boston Jah, how much do you pay for each kilo and where is it coming from, and tell us about the purity?"

Jah-key, as everybody called him, was from Boston. He pushed his long dreds back and contemplated whether he should answer the question. Jah-key debated with himself about the question then finally relented. "I'm acquiring them for twenty a piece and that's regardless if I buy 100 or 200... A Mexican Cartel is all I'm going to say about the source, and the purity is only sixty percent."

"You see what I'm saying... Their charging us top dollar for low quality material. There's no droughts, or major seizures that have occurred within the past few years. America is letting it in. So, why are we the ones who's getting jerked around here. They dictate the prices people." Naseem stopped to survey the room then continued.

"The Colombians are shipping these drugs to the middlemen. Ladies and gentlemen, for the same prices it was when we were younger or back in the good ol' days for some of us. The only thing now is that the middlemen are stepping on it and shipping it to us. The Colombian organizations don't have time to be stepping on it then charging these middlemen top dollar. No! They're business men who are trying to keep the flow moving and the money coming in...

"Now, the price and purity is the reason why cocaine is in the decline right now. These people are taking it back to the 70's era when kilos were going for 50,000 and the rich were only getting the drug." He shook his head. "No! No! No! Not on our watch!"

"So are these people here the only shareholders in this venture or are there others?" Crystal waved her manicured hand around the table. "And, what about background checks, the possible threats of local and state law enforcement? These things we need to know because everybody didn't come to power, as the common hood. A lot of us have legitimate businesses, families and are pillars in our respected communities. How do we keep our self insulated and layered from any dangers lurking on the horizon?"

Naseem strolled back over and took a seat with the rest of the group. All of Crystal questions were legitimate ones. He had outlined most of Crystal concerns in the prospectus that was laid out in front of everyone, but had yet to explain it.

"Excuse me, before you answer that, which I'm pretty sure is outlined in the folder, I wanted to know who do you deal with and who will be the number one supplier?" The whole group glanced down at Eric, who sat at the other end of the table. He was a Cali native. He'd been in the business for almost two decades. Eric had made a lot of money and invested most it into an exotic rental car business. He stayed in the Baldwin Hills section of Los Angles, dined with entertainers and politicians and had the backing of the notorious Piru Bloods. Eric, despite the high prices, still managed to place a ton of cocaine on the LA streets monthly. But, that might all be coming to an end. Eric dealt directly with Juan Guzman. The man who was now the current leader of the Sinaloa Cartel.

Juan Guzman had just been arrested and the LA streets had been dry. So, that meant that Eric would be in need of a new reliable supplier.

With the lost of Juan, Eric wanted to know who Naseem had in mind. There were only a few organizations that could provide that type of weight.

"The Matta family! The purity is at 90 percent right now and the price depends on what Port it goes through... So, they say. But folks... They own the Port of Balboa. They have direct access to the organization, who now is the number one producer of cocaine in Colombia. And, they also have the White Hand on their team... I'm sure everybody is familiar with them and the Freeway Ricky story. Well that's who's backing them and us if we decide to organize this here."

Eric smiled at the response. He was thrilled with Naseem's choice. Eric had done business with them before, but liked dealing with the Cartel better.

The Matta family and Sinaloa Cartel were the two competing sources for America's cocaine thirst. Both had the highly sophisticated Colombian sources and both had the same quality, at times, but the Matta family was business first. Where, the Sinaloa Cartel was violent and brought a lot of heat with them, and didn't have the backing of the CIA. Which was the downside of dealing with them.

"So people what do you think?" Naseem asked with his hands out.

Eric rose first and replied. "I'm in... I read the folder and I love the ideal. I love the ideal of these background checks."

"After careful consideration, I agree also... My team will be willing to provide this group with any support during the transitional period and I love the idea of working with the Matta family. They're respectable people and business minded like this group here."

One after the other, they started rising up from their seats and giving their approvals along with their support and resources to aid the plan. Naseem grinned, and after every pledge he gestured with a simple nod.

Destiny didn't budge. She was a newbie of some sort but came with high recommendations from some of the vets in the business. Destiny raised her hand. Everybody took a seat and waited for the coffee colored diva to speak.

She raised her head high, and displayed an aura of confidence before speaking her next word. "I have a concern... I'm pretty sure everybody here or most of the people here knows about my situation."

A few heads nodded around the room. She had been handpicked by some of these very people so it was known who Destiny was linked to and how deep her pockets were from them connections.

Naseem leaned back in the chair. He was one of the people to pick Destiny for the group. "What's your concern? And, please be blunt about it because if this is going to work... We need everybody's input."

"There was an attempt on my life." Destiny hung her head down, and tried to gather her courage. The event had been a traumatic one but proved to be a fruitful one. It was sort of like a blessing and curse. "Does anybody here deal with Alex Diaz?"

"Alex is a snitch!" Tony Rome from Las Vegas said. He had also been getting supplied by Alex. This was prior to Alex becoming a government witness. But, after word got out that Alex spilled his guts in a Philadelphia federal courtroom Tony Rome disappeared and scored cocaine elsewhere.

"That's the reason why I'm asking... This man, Alex, has ruined my family, and this here is how I was introduced to this life..." She glanced around the room before rising up from the chair.

Destiny had a slender frame, and the long-sleeveless white dress did its wonders. The exotic looking woman commanded attention, and why wouldn't she? Destiny was mixed of Arabian and Jamaican blood. "If I join this group and place my money in your hands..." Destiny stopped to let the words resonate through the old room. She stared at Naseem.

Naseem noticed the seriousness in Destiny's tone and demeanor but was distracted, just a little, by her beauty.

"I do not want to deal with this Matta family, if they're dealing with Alex or anybody that's associated with him... And, that goes for anybody in this group... No informants, cooperating witnesses or giving up anybody to help the law... I don't want to be a part of that, and I promised my team that they had my word on this... So, it's imperative that if you're on that or that's how you've gotten by for so long then I don't want to be a part of this here." Destiny said, forcing her strong Jamaican features out.

"Destiny, this is going to be a different situation then before... I promise this... Everybody gets full background checks, and this is on the State and federal level. We're striving to change that culture... Like I said before. This here is historic for a number of reasons, and that concern of yours is one of them."

Destiny nodded her head, yes. She took a seat, and eyed Naseem. Destiny was serious about this part. She wasn't going to get lured into the same trap that her boyfriend, Polo had got thrown into. Destiny wanted to win, and enjoy life to the fullest. Nothing else. She had come too far in life to let someone just take it away by a few simple words to the wrong people.

Naseem sat back and viewed the audience. The atmosphere felt great, and the group seemed willing to participate. Destiny words sunk deep in his heart. He understood the concerns, and was trying to avoid the same mistakes of so many others who had been involved in the business. And, one of the people who mistakes he tried to avoid was his brother, Titan.

Chapter 3

"Oh my God!" Brenda screamed then dropped the phone. Tears came down her chubby mulatto face. She couldn't believe it, and didn't want to believe it but it was true. Luis Matta was dead.

Brenda Matta sat by the window in the presidential place with her head on Sofia's shoulder. She couldn't compose herself. The reality of losing Luis was enormous. She had always known it was possible, especially with Luis dealing in the contraband business.

She tried to sway Luis away from it on numerous occasions. Even threatened to divorce him and shame the family. It was a lie and bogus. Brenda knew the business was the way of life in Panama. This was the very foundation on how the Matta brothers built their vast holdings.

She sobbed uncontrollable. Sofia rubbed her head and held Brenda tight. "It's going to be alright. I'm here for you... I'm here for you."

"No... No... No..." Brenda continued to grieve, and say between the sobs.

Sofia eyes also became watery. She was visibly distraught. Although older than Brenda, at 60, by two years Sofia still had the appearance of a woman in her early 40's. She also was a mulatto who didn't feel ashamed that her father was from West Africa, Mali. Sofia, as well as Brenda, embraced this part of their life.

Sofia was feeling the same pain that her baby sister felt. Luis Matta was family to her, and a very close friend. They all had grown up poor in the Santa Cruz section of Panama. She closed her eyes trying to gain some strength for Brenda.

It was hard though. Up to this point, in their adult lives, it was a carefree life for them. Brenda had Luis. He took care of everything. Brenda didn't have a big responsibility except taking care of their daughter, Bonita.

Sofia, on the other hand, struck gold. She married the future president of Panama. This chance meeting between Sofia and Richardo happened while attending college together. Richardo was a handsome man from Santa Ana. It's a well-to-do part of Panama City, and most of the families there had obtained wealth, either by legal or illegal means. And, the Ayala family got it both ways in the old days. It was different now. Richardo Ayala tried and managed to stay away from the illegal drug trade. Although, he did turn a blind eye to the Matta family dealings, and made sure the government did too.

The sisters managed to sit on the white leather sectional sofa. A vintage cocktail table sat in the middle of the sofa with a vase full of colorful flowers of all different sorts.

Upon hearing the news, beforehand by Richardo, Sofia had all the maids and houseworkers exit her personal quarters. Sofa didn't want the workers in the presidential palace to see Brenda have a nervous breakdown.

Brenda jolted up. She had just had an epiphany. Brenda realized what was going on, and why Luis had been murdered, or so she thought.

"Bonita... Bonita... Sofia, we have to tell Bonita that her father was murdered... He was murdered by them. Them, Americans who what to steal our business. We need to hurry and protect Bonita." She said with a little bit of black mascara running down her tanned round face.

Sofia understood her point. She quickly leaped up off the sofa, and snatched the phone off the sea grass rug.

"Richardo!" She yelled into the cell phone. It dialed the president's phone, and started to ring.

He answered on the third ring. "Si, Mommi."

"Poppi, Bonita! We need to find Bonita... She's in America."

Destiny

Chapter 4

The meeting had ended early and everybody departed, simultaneously, from the estate.

Limousines, trucks, SUVs, and other high-end foreign machines paraded down the back roads. Destiny's car was near the back of the pack. She rode in the back of a chauffeured, black, Maybach S600.

Destiny laid her head back on the soft leather headrest, and crossed her legs. The knee-high black Gucci boots complimented her coffee colored legs. But, the white Balmain mini-dress hid little. She didn't care. Hopefully, the driver was paying more attention to navigating the back roads of New York, and not underneath of her mini. Destiny had thought to herself.

"Destiny, we have a meeting at 6 with the lawyer." Meka stated without even staring at Destiny.

"Which lawyer is this one?" Destiny responded without lifting her head.

Meka flicked to the left on the phone for a second before finding what she was searching for. "Oh, I'm sorry... It's... It's the entertainment lawyer Martin Barzini."

"Oh..." Destiny said, not all that enthusiastic about meeting with him. She knew it was a priority though.

Destiny dreaded the meeting, and really didn't want to depart with that part of her life. But, she knew it was inevitable. She couldn't do both. Modeling was one thing, and took a great deal of her time. And, watching over the Jones Foundation was another.

Destiny didn't have time to wrestle with the situation. She didn't want to talk to Meka, her assistant. Nor did she feel like talking period.

Destiny needed time to think, and plan. She felt like everything was moving so fast, and out of control. But, it wasn't. Life was going her way, at this moment.

She harbored these thoughts while glancing at the passing farmlands, trees, and houses. She started to feel a lot of resentment from the situation that she had been thrust into.

Destiny shook her head, and stated out loud to herself. "This is all your fault Polo Jones."

* * *

The pool of green jumpsuits was scattered around the small room. Girlfriends, baby mommas, mothers, and home boys sat across the miniature table from their incarcerated loved ones. Three Correctional Officers were reclined behind a four-foot desk situated at the front of the room.

Polo was relaxed in his prison issue green. He waited patiently for his visit. Polo remained stressed from the testimony he had given a couple days before. He wished at this moment in life that he'd never done such a stupid thing, let alone to his brother. Polo even contemplated suicide for his vicious betrayal of loyalty to Priest.

Destiny strolled through the main entrance like she was God's gift. She wore her hair down in a sophisticated fashion. The long black silky hair draped on her shoulders, which allowed her strong Jamaican facial features to be noticeable. She headed straight to the desk where the lazy guards were seated and asked, "Is Polo Jones down already?" The guard rose up, and pointed in the direction of where he was seated. She strolled off towards his direction. Everybody's attention was focused, on the pretty woman, who wore a black chic lingerie type top with red slim-fit chic pants. She was used to the lustful stares and comments of men and women when appearing anywhere. Destiny thrived off of that attention, which was why she loved modeling so much.

Polo watched the stares, as his eye catcher headed down the row of seats and tables. Destiny sensed Polo's stares, so she put an extra twist in her step just like he always loved her to do. He stood up when Destiny approached his seat. The two hugged, kissed, and took a seat together.

"Hey, baby, I miss you!"

"I miss you too, sweetheart," Polo said smiling, truly missing her.

"Polo. They found Priest guilty this morning," Destiny said, with a sad tone, then dropped her head down. She loved Priest and was upset when Polo told her that he had to snitch on him. Destiny tried to talk him out of it, and he even reconsidered it numerous times until Rita had made it clear to him. Priest or no deal.

"I heard... It was on the news."

Destiny raised her head, and tried to put a smile on her face, but it was hard.

"So how you been?" Polo asked, while he rubbed her face.

"Guess what?"

"What?"

"I made the cover of Vogue... London!"

"That's big."

"And I waited to tell you this in person," she said, elated. "I just signed a contract to be the face of Tracy Reese."

Destiny, at the urging of Polo, worked hard on her career, and it paid off. She traveled extensively and came into contact with a lot of major players in the fashion world. After a major show in Paris the designer Tracy Reese approached Destiny about helping her expand the Tracy Reese brand. Destiny accepted the opportunity without thinking twice.

Tracy Reese was legendary, an icon and had it rough, as she tried to establish herself in the fashion world. She finally broke into the secluded fashion world, which shunned African-American designers, by having the opportunity to design a dress for Michelle Obama's private birthday party. Destiny loved her achievements, dedication, and determination so she agreed to represent Tracy Reese's brand.

Polo was ecstatic about the news and said, "I'm proud of you."

"You made it all possible. I wish we could go celebrate together," she said, sadly.

"Don't worry. I'll be there in due time."

Destiny glanced off, and looked around at all the different prisoners in the room. She still was upset about Priest not being able to come home. Destiny tried to remain quiet about it, especially in front of Polo. She knew he still was dealing with issues of Priest's fate.

"What about Priest? We got to help him. Priest always been good to me. I love him... That's my big brother," Destiny said, not caring about how he felt about being silent on the issue.

"Don't worry! I'm going to get him home. He just got to sit for a little bit... That's all."

He really didn't mean it, at that particular moment. Polo was upset by what Priest had done recently.

* * *

A tear dropped down from her eye. That had been the last visit she had with Polo. It wasn't the last meeting because of his vicious betrayal to Priest but for the reason of her almost being killed.

"Meka, please give me a tissue."

She reached into Destiny's Prada clutch, and retrieved a few tissues. Meka didn't ask any questions or make any suggestions. She had been

Destiny's personal assistant going on two years now. So, it wasn't unusual for Destiny to get depressed, at times, and to start tearing for nothing. At least that's what Meka thought. Destiny had never told Meka about the incident, and wasn't planning on telling Meka either. It was a private matter, and only those who were involved knew about it.

Destiny grabbed the tissue without turning towards the round face girl. She patted her eyes lightly, and tried not to smear any of the make-up.

* * *

The wind blew cold air fast and hard out of the vent, high above the cell making a hissing sound. Which made the twelve-by-seven cell colder than ever. Situated against the back wall were two metal-framed bunk beds with thin mats covering the beds. Priest garbed in a green jumpsuit stood up leaning on the metal beds frame with a USA Today paper open in his hands. "Online poker company swiftly clears 100 million in revenues in the third quarter," Priest said aloud to himself, as he quoted exactly what the paper wrote. He was happy, and mad. He just shook his head at the unbelievable gain of his company.

Priest was infuriated with Polo and Alex's actions. He was determined to make them feel the same pain he did. While he waited for trial, Priest befriended Abdul Walid, who was locked up for a gun charge and was only looking at five years. The two got real close and gained each other's trust, so Priest asked Walid for a favor.

Abdul Walid was no slouch. He came up in Chester getting money and killing. Walid was down for whatever, but wasn't a fool by far though. He moved cautiously with his crew and never really did business, such as hits or murders for anyone. But Priest was different.

After Polo took the stand, Priest made his mind up. He came back from court and pulled Walid in the cell. Priest had explained to Walid that he had a problem and that he would put a million dollars apiece on two people heads. He needed Walid's partners to kill Destiny and Alex's young wife, Izmir. Walid agreed to help him out, and he' got the message out to his people. Priest was thrilled. So with a little down payment the deal was sealed.

Even though he regretted doing it, Priest convinced himself that Destiny had to go. No matter how much love he had for her, Priest knew that that was the only way he could settle the score with Polo.

Priest had watched faithfully, as Destiny arrived at the jail on Thursdays to come visit Polo. It was like clockwork. Destiny only missed her visits when she had work overseas, so he laid out a plan for Walid's crew to follow. Priest wanted them to follow Destiny from the visit, and kill her. Period. Point blank.

"Knock! Knock!" sounded the metal door. An inmate stood outside the cell door. Priest glanced up, and waved for the man to come inside. Walid stepped inside wearing a cream colored thermal shirt with some gray sweatpants and black boots.

"What's up, old head?" Walid asked.

"Ya people's on top of that?" He got straight to the point.

"They waiting outside now."

"Oh aight! I'm going to get my girl to send that money now," Priest said, then smiled at the thought.

Destiny strutted outside to the parking lot. She didn't have a care in the world and still high off of the visit with Polo. He completed her, and Destiny had vowed to stick by him. No matter what the circumstances were, Destiny would be in Polo's corner. And, why wouldn't she be. Polo was the one who introduced her to an elegant and classy lifestyle and who made the call to Top Notch agency, and got her the modeling deal that changed her life drastically. Destiny owed Polo her life and loyalty, and she wasn't going to compromise on either one.

She reached the white Range Rover. She got in the SUV, and started it up. Destiny yanked out of the parking lot, and pulled into the Market Street traffic. It was kinda light for the night but a few cars and trucks still filled the four lane street.

A tinted-up burgundy Crown Victorian, kept a little distance, but still paced the Range Rover.

Destiny was flying through the Philly streets. She had planned to stay for a few days then head back to her condo in New York. She hated staying in the city after Polo got arrested, and couldn't wait to leave Philly.

She made it out of Center City, and flew down Broad Street towards the North side of Philly. She was catching all the green lights down the long strip. Destiny caught the light at Broad and Leigh, and stopped then bobbed a little bit to the music.

The Crown Vic pulled, slowly, behind the Range. Destiny checked her rear-view mirror, and noticed the burgundy squatter for the first time. She didn't pay it any mind. The light switched again, and Destiny banged off to the right on Leigh Avenue riding down Leigh Avenue was like going into another world. The natives called this part, The Badlands. It was called this for its notorious reputation of violence, and open drug markets. If you wanted it, they had it. From guns to drugs, and even hired guns for murder. The area was predominantly Puerto Rican but there was a sprinkle of blacks here and there.

The Badlands was buzzing today. People were out and about on this hot summer night. They walked up and down the filthy strip and clustered blocks.

Destiny rode down the street. She was heading for Delaware Ave, in order to a make a stop. She had to gas up and meet one of Polo's friends, Major, before heading to Polo's house.

She made it to the end of Leigh Avenue and rode under the train tracks. Destiny debated with herself on whether to pull into the gas station that sat on the corner. It wasn't a busy station but mostly young hitters stopped there before heading into the Badlands and some even met their out of town customers there to conduct business. Polo had always warned her about these type of places. Philly was a dangerous place and there was always a person searching for the next lick.

Destiny, thought for a second, but decided against it. It wasn't safe enough. She was a woman, at night, in a Range Rover, and not familiar with all the crooks and criminals that roamed Philly, she decided against it. Destiny road ahead, and hit Delaware Avenue. A well-lit gas station sat right at the intersection. She pulled in front a pump. Coastal wasn't crowded and only a few cars were in front of the pumps. Nobody was pumping gas. Everybody was in the store buying goodies and other things. She sat in the SUV for a minute, in order to gather her things, before getting out and heading in the store.

The Crown Vic pulled in a few seconds after Destiny. She seen the vehicle pull in the station but just thought it was a coincidence.

"Damn, shorty bad as a mutha fucka! Them red pants are fitting that tight little ass." The young hitter, Meer said.

"Yo, she definitely bad... Did he say we could fuck her? " Idris said, while eyeing Destiny walking into the station.

"No, you nutt-ass nigga! Yo, man ain't nobody hitting shit. My nigga, we came to do a job, and that's what we going to do... Remember, nigga! Damn, you niggas always got pussy on y'all minds… This, our shot at some real paper." Hak blasted before hitting the Dutch again.

The three-man crew were blowing on some loud. This was their normal routine. Riding around blowing on loud and plotting on the next lick. Not on no petty licks but on some nice size jobs but lately they been on slumping niggas.

The trio were all from the Highland Gardens section of Chester. Everybody in the city called this domain 'Killa Hill', and these three represented Killa Hill to the fullest.

Lately, they had been on a mission. Bricks of cocaine were in the high 40s, nobody really had money these days, and all the young gangstas in Chester were on killing sprees. So the group was on the same shit. Catching bodies were on their plate at the time, and their comrade Abdul Walid knew this so he sent some work their way.

"Idris, yo, we not going to hit her out here... Go, see if the door is open and, if so, jump in the backseat on her ass."

Idris leaped out the back of the car. A bunch of smoke flew in to the air, as the door swung open. Nobody stared though, a few people were at the pump now but were minding their business, and didn't bother to pay attention to the short gangster.

The young hitter was light in the rear. He weighed 140 pounds soak and wet. The loud had a hold on the youngster, and he treated the habit well.

Idris pulled his all black Sixers hat low over his brown face then hung his head low. Idris didn't want his face caught on tape and blasted across Instagram for this crime. He was a veteran at this. Idris already had two bodies under his belt that had occurred in less than 18 months. So, he knew how to creep. He was dressed in a black t-shirt that had Killa Hill written in white letters, black denim GBS jeans and tan Timbs.

Idris lifted his head for a second to see how close he was to the SUV. He stepped up to the passenger door then grabbed the handle and pulled. The door didn't budge. It was locked. He swung around to the driver side door and yanked the door open.

"Bet! He got it open." Meer said while leaned up in the front seat window of the Crown Vic. He hit the Dutch again in order to confirm his happiness before passing it off to Hak.

Idris leaped in the Range and closed the door behind. He jumped in the backseat, right behind the driver seat and sat low.

Destiny strolled outside the store clutching a small black tote bag in one hand, and keys in the other.

Idris seen her coming and ducked in the seat. Destiny went to the pump, and started filling the truck up. She glanced around, sang a short song to herself then finished filling the tank up.

Destiny opened the door and flopped in the seat. She didn't bother to turn around or even look out of the rear-view mirror. Destiny started the truck, and Beyonce's song *Single Ladies* played at a low tone, before she pulled off.

"Damn, I hope he just kill the bitch, and get it over with." Meer was mad. He didn't feel like all this kidnapping stuff. He had other plans for the night, and murder was one and banging his young girl out was the other.

"Yo, he can't kill her while the fucking truck is moving. You nutt-ass nigga!"

"Nigga stop calling me a nutt-ass nigga too!" Meer wasn't trying to hear Hak shit tonight.

"Matter of fact, text that nigga, and tell him to make that bitch pull over in one of those backstreets in the Badlands... Fuck it; kill that bitch up here so they can find her in Philly."

Meer hurried and sent the text.

Idris waited for a second. Destiny had just pulled out of the Coastal, and was on Delaware Avenue.

Idris leaped forward and brandished the .40 caliber at Destiny then slammed the nozzle in the back of her head.

Destiny swerved into the right lane nearly hitting a few cars. "Oh God! No please, no!"

"Shut up bitch and don't fucking crash the truck... Just drive until I say so..."

"Okay! Okay!" Destiny screamed with tears falling from her face.

26

Idris felt his phone vibrate. He snatched it out of his pocket and seen it was a text from Meer. He read it then shook his head.

"Yo, bitch turn this mutha fucka around and head back to SA land..."

Destiny had already sped down Delaware Ave and was darn near by the onramp to 195 South. "I can't... I can't... I'm going to have to..." She couldn't get the thought out. Destiny mind was racing. She was thinking of survival, and turning around going into the vicious Badlands wasn't a good idea.

She drove onto the ramp and got on the highway.

"Didn't I tell ya dumb ass to turn around? Aight then I'm going to fuck you then kill ya dumb ass tonight. I wasn't going to hurt you but ya ass don't listen."

Idris raised the phone to his mouth and yelled. "Killa Hill!" Meer, immediately picked the phone up off the first ring. "What's up nigga! Why the fuck you get on the highway?"

"Man this bitch ain't fucking listening... I swear I'm 'bout to drop her right here." Idris stated then jammed the barrel in the back of Destiny head.

"Naw we taking that bitch to the City... Get off at the Eastside exit."

"Aight..." Idris replied then hung up on Meer.

The Range Rover sped down 195 doing 70 mph. Hak stayed on their tail in the Crown Vic. The crew was furious. Their plan was falling apart, and they needed to improvise. The Killa Hill crew was good at it though. They thought, quickly, on their feet.

Finally, they made it to Chester. Destiny took the first exit leading to the poverty-stricken City of Chester.

It was extremely dark on the side street. Idris acted quickly. He knew this was the best time to take control of the situation. No police was around, and they were in the middle of the slums. Even, if he had to down her right there, nobody would be able to witness the murder.

He grabbed Destiny's neatly done hair that was tucked up in a bun, and twisted it hard. "Pull over bitch, now!"

Destiny swerved over to the side but didn't let her foot off the gas.

"Place, this mutha fucka in park!" Idris barked at her.

Destiny parked the truck. Hak slid directly on the side of the Range Rover. Meer leaped out of the Crown Vic, and snatched the door open.

"No! No... Please, I'll give you anything. Money, I got it... Please don't." Destiny screamed waving blows at Meer. She was loud but nobody could hear the cries. There were row homes lined up across the street but were deserted. Destiny was all alone with these mass-murders.

Idris gripped Destiny by the hair and yanked her in the back of the Range. Meer slid in the driver's seat and sped off. They drove straight to Killa Hill, and parked in front of an abandoned house on Honan Street. Destiny was dragged into a piss and vermin infested dilapidated house that had no front door, backdoor and the roof was halfway gone. The open space brought the star-filled night into the house. It was a dangerous place. The hired hitters didn't care. This was the same place that they took, willingly, teenage girls and broke they virginity.

Destiny was tied up and thrown on the ground. Meer stood in front of her with a chrome-plated .45 Ruger. But before he fired the shot, the crew heard footsteps outside of the house.

Jay and Tate stormed through the door. The two six footers looked like professional basketball players but they weren't. They were gangsters.

The youngsters froze for a second but then chilled when they seen the old heads coming through the door.

"Naw, ya niggas drawing... Ain't no killing up in these jawns no more... Plus, I need her. My peoples sent me to get her." Jay snapped out and said.

The young Killa Hill boys were in a dilemma. Destiny had a hundred thousand dollars on her head, or so they thought. It was really a million dollars but Abdul Walid wasn't given them that much. He needed a break down too. But, the youngsters needed the money no matter how much it was.

"Ae, Old head... You know the situation with the jawn. Her peoples are rats. Plus, the bul gave us the go on her." Hak spoke up for the group.

"Yeah, I know the whole situation with the jawn but he called it off... This my man peoples and she ain't no snitch. It's her bitch-ass boyfriend... Not her. So, we're taking her with us."

Tate didn't bother to hear a reply from the boys. He started untying Destiny, and managed to help her up.

Everybody just stood around in the smelly house staring at Destiny. She was beautiful and now she would be safe. God had definitely answered her silent prays.

The call had come down. Destiny wasn't supposed to be killed, and she was saved in the nick of time.

Hak glanced around and signaled for his little crew to go. They understood what had just happened, and respected the call and didn't second guess it coming from the two brothers. And, why would they. These two men were killers. The original members of the infamous 'Boyle Street Boys.' The group that the name 'Killa Hill' was derived from. They had dropped so many bodies up the Highland Gardens and around the city that they were considered true 'Living Legends' in the City.

All of this fame came with a cost though. They had just been released from federal prison. This was due to a scandal that broke out in the

Chester Police Department.

The brothers had been arrested in February of 2003. A federal grand jury had indicted them, and eight others on a 44-count indictment that consisted of Racketeering, Murder, Tampering with a Witness By Murder, and drug charges.

The case gained a lot of press and the Attorney General in Washington, DC authorized the death penalty for them.

Jay, Tate and their other co-defendant named Dre took them to trial. They lost but the jury declined to kill the young men. All three of them were sentenced to three life sentences plus 30 years without parole.

They appealed, and appealed for years, but the courts denied every motion filed. That was until the Feds investigated the Chester Police Department. The Feds exposed a lot of corruption and mishandling of evidence in numerous cases. This provided the brothers with a way out. Dre wasn't able to get out on this. He had a murder that wasn't investigated by the Chester Police, so that conviction was good to uphold his sentence. But, he would gain his freedom by another avenue.

Jay and Tate were released from prison. Dre remained in the joint but was about get a sentence reduction.

The reduction Dre was waiting on stemmed from a Supreme Court decision called, Miller v Alabama where the court said that you couldn't give a defendant who committed murder as a teenager a mandatory life sentence. But, that's just what they had done with Dre.

Tate helped Destiny out of the abandoned house. She was grateful that these two men had just come to rescue her. She thanked them repeatedly. Destiny felt that their bravery had earned them her loyalty and she planned to show them that.

After exchanging numbers, Destiny promised to stay in touch with the brothers.

* * *

"Destiny, the phone is for you." Meka said trying to take Destiny out of her daydream.

"Who is it? I told you that I wasn't taking any calls."

"Oh, it's Major... I thought you said if he called, you're always available." Meka responded with a confused mug on her face.

"I'm sorry Meek. I'm not myself today... It's alright I'll take Major call." Destiny said with a slight smile then grabbed the phone out of her hand. "Maj, how you been today?"

"I'm good... How everything work out?"

Chapter 5

Large banners read: FAMM Thank You For 25 years of Service To The People. A few of these banners hung on the opposite sides of the large center and one large banner sat in the background above the stage.

A crowd of about 5,000 filled the DC Convention center. It was the 25th anniversary of the advocacy group called, Families Against Mandatory Minimums and the organization threw a huge party in the Nation's Capital. Just to say thank you to its founder, and everybody else that made the organization a force to be reckoned with.

A lot of great people were in attendance. Lawyers, ex-convicts, other advocacy groups, freedom fighters from around the country and some important officials that worked in the White House.

Julia Stewart, the founder of FAMM, wanted to do it big for the event and draw some much needed attention to the incarceration issue. And, this was a good way to brand the ideal on a huge level.

This issue was relevant to a good portion of the country because mass-incarceration was an enormous problem. The nation had close to 2 million of its own citizens locked away in dangerous jails and prisons across the country. And, more than half of those 2 million were either non-violent drug offenders or drug addicts that made a fatal mistake of trying to hustle in order to take care of their drug addiction, and some were labeled both.

America was incarcerating its citizens at an alarming rate and the people of America, of all colors, race, and creed; were finally waking up and taking notice of this vicious trend.

Lana Davis was a part of this elaborate event. She had been invited by Julia Stewart, herself, and was asked to speak. Lana kindly accepted Julia's initiation.

The mission and goal to end mass incarceration meant a lot to Lana. It was near and dear to her heart. Lana had, at one point, been a victim of this horrific epidemic.

Lana was just 20 years old when she was sentenced to 40 years in federal prison for a drug crime that she didn't even commit.

The crime was for aiding and abetting a Racketeering enterprise that sold close to 200 kilograms of cocaine within a two year span.

At trial, the Government claimed that the enterprise was run by her boyfriend, Titan Gordon, and that Lana organized young women to drive vans and SUVs from Houston, Texas with cocaine in hidden stash spots to Pennsylvania for distribution to other drug dealers in the area.

This accusation was uttered throughout Lana's trial, even though none of the young ladies who got indicted testified or even cooperated with the government.

The government indicted 10 people and none of them cooperated with the DEA. It was a rare thing but it happened.

Lana was found guilty. She had exercised her Sixth Amendment right to a trial by her so-called peers. Even though, most of the jurors were older white men and women. She didn't have one black juror for her trial. Lana paid dearly for her decision to go to trial, and challenge the government's opinion that she was guilty of these crimes. The court handed down a hefty 40 year sentence.

Titan didn't fare better. He received a life sentence for being the leader and organizer of the group.

It wasn't long after her conviction that the case gained attention from some outside groups. Julia Stewart was one of them and came to Lana's rescue. FAMM pushed hard for the court to overturn Lana's conviction and sentence but all of that failed.

Luckily for Lana, her case garnered a lot of media attention and her sentenced was eventually commuted by President Obama in 2012. At the time of her release, Lana had served over 12 years in prison. Shortly after her release, Lana founded the non-profit Well-Wishers. This organization was founded to bring attention to other individuals who were serving harsh and illegal prison sentences. But, lately Lana was more concerned with getting Titan out of prison.

"Thank you." The crowd went wild and gave Lana a standing ovation. She gave a powerful speech about fighting for the long forgotten. "Thank you for understanding my story."

Lana was beaming, as she stepped off the stage, and headed to take a seat in the front. She was a beautiful lady. Lana strutted down the walkway in a black, shoulder less, evening gown with red Louis Vitton stilettos.

The young woman had come a long way and she realized it too. But, life wasn't complete without the love of her life.

After coming home from prison, Lana vowed to Titan that she would wait for him. Titan didn't want her to. He figured that his life was over. All of his appeals were done. President Obama had already stated that he wasn't letting any kingpins, leaders or major drug traffickers out of prison. So, Titan figured his chances were slim to be released.

The petite dark-skinned woman wouldn't settle for this. Lana wasn't accepting the fact that Titan was giving up hope. She couldn't. Titan was her first love, and first real relationship. They had been together since their junior high school years, and were inseparable ever since.

Titan had always been her rock growing up, and now she would be his.

The lovely sister smiled to the familiar faces in the crowd and waved a bit. Lana's pearly whites gleamed which complimented her radiant smile and beautiful attitude. She was a star that shined brightly. No matter who or what that tried to dim it.

Lana pushed her long black hair behind her shoulders and stood next to the attractive Bonita Matta.

Bonita was smiling and tears almost squeezed out of her exotic green eyes. She fought them back though, and kept her composure. She had been standing and clapping as Lana strutted down the walkway leading to the row. She stopped clapping when Lana got close enough to her then embraced her with a tight sisterly hug. Bonita was proud of her friend. She witnessed first-hand how much this cause meant to Lana, and planned on donating an enormous amount of money to Lana's non-profit company.

Bonita also understood the struggle. Although, she didn't personally, grow up like Lana or any of the other people that Lana named in her speech. She heard Naseem touch on it, almost daily, at home.

Lana took a seat but the crowd continued to clap. Bonita stood there and towered over the small woman.

The crowd finally stopped when the host walked across the stage to continue the event, and to bring the next speaker out.

Bonita rubbed the back of her red satin Versace gown, in order to take a seat. The fire truck red gown bought out the butterscotch complexion, and true inner sexiness of the Panamanian woman. She sat back and tried to focus on the man who just announced that his practice was in criminal justice. But before Bonita could hone in on what the man was saying, she saw one of her assistant's sneaking over with a phone in her hand.

Bonita didn't budge. She felt a little angry because the lady knew the rules. She stared at her walking fast, in a kneeled over position.

Paris, the assistant, didn't say a word. She just handed Bonita the phone. Bonita wouldn't take it. It was strict rules by the party promoters that no phones were allowed on while the party was going on.

"It's urgent... Ms. Matta sent this text." Paris said.

Bonita glanced around for a second then grabbed the phone. She went straight to the text that had just been sent.

"Your father and uncle were just murdered by the Americans!" The text read across the screen of Bonita's, iPhone.

She couldn't believe it, but it was true. Bonita dropped the phone on the ground and doubled over to cry.

Lana didn't understand what had just happened and stared at Paris like what's going on.

Paris snatched the phone off the ground then waved for Lana to get Bonita and come out to the hall.

Lana stood up, discretely, and tried to get Bonita who was so distraught that she didn't know what to do but follow Lana's lead to get up. But she couldn't.

Bonita was devastated and scared. She understood what had just happened. Luis and Pedro had been waiting for this day, and had been molding Bonita for years if this was to ever occur.

But no matter how much preparation she had for this unfortunate day, Bonita still couldn't, believe that it actually happened like her father predicted it would.

"The CIA really killed my father..." Bonita said, to herself while still bent over in a fetal position. She gathered herself together and stormed out of the room.

The Matta family legacy was at stake. The family fortunes were going to be up for grabs or rather the illegal side of things. The CIA wanted a part of the port and they killed the Matta brothers to show how serious they were about it.

Bonita was determined to stand up and be strong. But, she was the next target.

Chapter 6

The night was full of gloom. Storm clouds filled the sky. But it was no match for the beefy and elegant Sonoma, which soared through the air and commanded the upmost respect from Mother Nature's forceful power. The nose of the jet sliced through the clouds like a runaway slave dashing through the backwoods of Jamestown in Virginia. It had already traveled through the worst of it. There had been thunder storms fifty-miles back but it proved no match for the metal bird. Now, nothing but thick clouds lay ahead and stood in the way of the jet's destination.

Bonita had a window seat. She sat there, still in shock, peering out at the dark clouds. She was devastated by the betrayal; the treacherous act of the very same people that they had invited into their country. The news of the murders was hard for her to bear. But, she had to keep her sanity and take control of the dreadful circumstances.

She lifted the glass cup filled with cognac to her mouth, in a slow motion. Bonita was trying to figure it out. *Did they really kill Papi? Who made the call? Luis and Pedro weren't the type of men who you could just kill without first receiving confirmation.* These last few thoughts bothered her deeply.

A small drip of the expensive brown substance fell on Bonita's lap. She still had the fire engine red gown on. It was an expensive piece that Bonita loved because it brought out her inner beauty and lovable personality.

Paris leaped up from her seat and grabbed the cotton napkin that was lying on the wood grained table next to her laptop. She tipped over her bottle of water then wet the napkin and went to wipe the spot.

"NO! Leave it..."

Paris just stared for a second but didn't pay the order no mind. The gown was expensive and Bonita would regret the stain later and Paris knew this. Paris stormed over and cleaned the area while Bonita continued to stare out in space. She finished then went back towards her cushioned leather seat. Paris threw the napkin on the table and took a seat while pulling down her black miniskirt.

The luxury machine was decked out. It had a small leather sofa to the right and four single seats that could perform a full 360 motion, by the windows to the left of the jet. Each tan colored seat had a polished wooden table in front of it, and a 40 inch flat screen television was suspended in the air near the bathroom and kitchen entrance, which was located towards the back of the Sonoma.

Only the two pilots accompanied Bonita and Paris on the flight. No security, no kids, no maids, or other domestic help flew with them. The flight had been reserved for just the two. Bonita didn't want the company. She needed the space to think and plan, in order to execute her next move. At the request of Brenda, upon hearing the news she called Paris and had her prepare the long flight home for Bonita.

Being a great assistant and loyal friend, Paris did just that. She made all the calls then arranged for Bonita's security and other tag-alongs to fly in a separate privately-charted jet to Panama. They would meet up back in the old country.

Before leaving the States, Bonita had notified Naseem of the crazy twist of fate that had just swooped into her lap. He begged Bonita to come home and wait for a few days before going back to Panama. They needed to assess the situation and make the best educated move together.

Naseem let her know about all the important things that she was leaving behind, if she didn't think things through beforehand. Bella, their four year old daughter, him, and several other business, and social ventures that needed her immediate supervision. All of this needed her attention because the Matta family had major investments in America too. And, these investments and business relationships with these other owners and suppliers needed Bonita's assurance that everything would remain intact despite the unfortunate circumstances. This rung true even for her family that she just up and left, at a moment's notice.

When all of this failed, Naseem begged her to come home so that he could, at least depart with her. He wanted to protect his fiancé and family. His main concern was Bonita's safety, at this touchy time.

We had already formed an idea on how this would play out. Naseem was educated and had the street-smarts to match it. A rare combination for a native of Chester. Naseem knew how the cold world operated, and he didn't want it working its way into his family's home. That life and memory of poverty and death was behind him now. And, Naseem planned on keeping it that way, if he had the power to do so. But, somebody was for the Matta's fortune, business, or something. He couldn't wrap his mind around it yet because it was still in the beginning stage. The wolf or wolves were going to show their teeth soon enough when the appropriate time arrived. But, Bonita was directly in the middle of this. She was the only eligible sibling to take control of the whole operation. From the importing and exporting drugs all the way down to the business of selling the Matta's family commodity BANANAS.

Bonita disregarded all of his concerns; a lot of them had a ring of truth to them. She was her father's daughter. A true daddy's girl, as some called it.

Luis had already explained to her the significance of such a move. And, that if it was to happen, Bonita was to go directly to Panama City. Luis told her it was important to show strength, resilience, and organizational skills. That's why Panama City was the place she needed to show it at. Panama City was the center of power for the Matta's, and the family's illicit importing and exporting business.

The Matta family was powerful. This was so, even with the assass-ination of the brothers. They controlled all of the illegal commerce coming and going out of the Balboa Port.

Bonita slammed the glass down on the table. A splash of dark cognac landed on the cream, fluffy carpet.

Paris sat, directly facing Bonita on the flight. She had a laptop wide open and hitting away at the keys before the slight interruption. Paris had been busy at work. She was organizing the security and everybody else that Bonita Matta would need in place upon arriving in the country.

The woman was fiercely smart, much like Bonita. They both attended the Ivy League school called Stanford together where they were roommates. They became good friends or more like sisters.

Despite the fact that Paris could have gone and ran any Fortune 500 company, she remained with Bonita. Paris was loyal and dependable when it came to helping Bonita do anything. Paris knew the family background and reputation but she seen a better opportunity by working for the Matta family. Not only was she Bonita's assistant, Paris held the "chief financial officer" title in most of Bonita's companies. A title and position that brought in a multi-million dollar salary, and a lot of power and respect around the business sector in America and abroad.

Bonita had startled Paris a bit with the slamming of the glass. Paris stopped, in mid-tap of the key, and glanced at Bonita. "What's wrong? What do you need me to do?"

Bonita's mind had went blank during the early phase of the news then just like any intelligent person when under pressure, she remembered what Luis told her to do. "Get Omar Mossack on the phone..."

"Done. I already sent a text to him and informed him that you wanted a meeting tomorrow but I could demand his appearance tonight, if you like."

"Send a car out to get him. I want him to be waiting at the hanger upon my arrival... Let, Omar know it's extremely important. He knows by now my father was murdered. He will understand the urgency of the meeting."

Paris shook her head. She was working under extreme pressure at the moment. The stakes were high. Her life, livelihood and best friend existence depended on the next few decisions that were being made.

* * *

"We're business first, beautiful butterfly." Luis rubbed Bonita's slim face, with the back of his soft hand, as he glared into Bonita's green eyes and called her the childhood name that he had given her. "Omar Mossack should be the very first person you meet before moving on to make any decisions... The family's interest is the first concern before anything... We can't be selfish. The Matta's have massive holdings here and abroad beautiful. A lot of people depend on us, and Omar Mossack will make sure that it stays that way... He's an honorable and loyal man. I, and your uncle Pedro, trust his judgment." Luis then pointed at Bonita. "But, that's because he fears me and Pedro!" Luis said sternly while pointing to make his point. "Fear is always better than love... Fear is always better than love... Fear is always better than love, Bonita... Fear is your companion, friend, and executor. When the time comes he has to fear you also, if you want to keep this family alive."

* * *

Bonita remembered the words of her father like it was just yesterday. They had been riding through the business district of New Orleans on St. Charles Avenue. Where they stopped to walk-thru and check on Luis tropical fruit company called United Brands. Throughout the whole day, Luis had been talking and drilling nothing but the family's history and business dealings into her head. Bonita didn't understand why her father would be telling her these things. At the time, Bonita had just graduated from Balboa Academy when she was at the tender age of seventeen.

Luis knew she was smart for her age, and had even more potential with the right guidance. Therefore, the private school gave her a start with an excellent education that revolved around an American AP Program. Luis would follow this up by enrolling her into Stanford. Which could provide that perfect edge for her then he would lay out the path of success for her.

She loved him for the advice and help. Now, Bonita would have to muster the courage and intelligence to make it work.

"We have security picking up Mr. Mossack up, as we speak... I just got the text." Paris said, without taking her eyes off the screen.

"How long until we land?"

"Maybe twenty minutes... Would you like to change? I have your evening clothes packed in the back storage."

"I'm fine... Did you notify my mother that I was coming?"

"Yes."

"Is she still at the presidential palace?"

"Yes... Mrs. Matta is still there, and has been assigned security by the president."

"Why is there none of the family's detail there?"

"They were all removed by President Ayala until further notice... For Mrs. Matta's safety, at least until everything is sorted out."

"Who made the decision!?"

"The President..."

Bonita didn't bother to question her any further. She knew that her mother was scared and didn't have any faith in nobody except her family right now.

The Sonoma made a nice landing despite the fact that it was raining hard.

The air traffic crew at Tocumen International Airport guided the jet to a private 3,600 square foot hangar. This was the family's domain. As the jet rolled into the hanger, six black Tahoe's followed the Sonoma to its final stop. The jet came to a halt. Armed men leaped out of the SUV's wearing black business suits and toting assault rifles.

Bonita had a clear view of the action taking place outside of her window. The men appeared tough and had an aggressive demeanor about them. They seemed like they were ready and alert for the job. *But were they?* Bonita had this thought in the back of her head. It was the thought that she carried with her throughout the whole flight. These were men, who were similar to the trained men that had let Luis and Pedro get mowed down.

The stairs came down from the Sonoma and two of the men darted up the steps. Paris greeted them at the door. "Hi, Hector and Miguel... Ms. Matta is in the back. She wants Mr. Mossack to come up and speak with her."

"Si..." They said, simultaneously, then Hector turned and spoke into his sleeve, in Spanish.

One of the armed guards tapped on the tinted out window.

Omar Mossack stepped out of the vehicle. He didn't appear much like an attorney who ran the fourth largest law firm that specialized in creating offshore accounts and businesses. Omar created shell companies that provided multiple layers of protection, in order to hide hundreds of millions.

Omar walked with a slight wobble due to the protruding stomach that fell over onto his tan khaki pants. He wore a striped blue shirt with suspenders and a navy blue overcoat to match. Omar had curly gray hair that he combed to the back, and appeared every bit of the 62 years of age that he was despite the chubby, clean shaven face. This might have been because Omar wore old gold framed glasses.

He glanced around the hanger while making his way to the G5. Omar appeared concerned. He didn't know what was going on or why Bonita had called him at such an unexpected time of the night demanding a meeting.

Omar stepped through the doorway. Paris was there waiting then pointed towards the back. "This way Mr. Mossack... Ms. Matta is waiting in the lounge area."

"Si..."

Omar headed towards Bonita. She sat in the chair with her hands folded and legs tightly crossed. Bonita was all business at this point. This wasn't a formal meeting but a business one. So power and confidence had to dominate her demeanor and approach.

She didn't bother to stand when Omar Mossack reached her area, as was custom.

He extended his hand before greeting Bonita, "Hi, Ms. Matta... My condolences go out to you and the family on the loss of my friends, Luis and Pedro."

Bonita accepted the handshake. "Thank you... Mr. Mossack... Please have a seat." She waved Omar over to the leather sectional.

"My father and uncle were murdered today... At this time, I have a clue but I'm not for certain who did this," she explained and revealed a little bit of her hand.

The old man gave a hunch with his shoulders like he didn't know either."I don't understand..."

Bonita held up her manicured, French vanilla tipped finger in order to stop Omar's response. "You may not know or you may... But, I will seek revenge for this dreadful act. The party who did this will be held accountable for these murders... Without any questions."

"Si.."

"Now, I want to make sure the family business matters are secure and that nobody has tried to make a move on anything."

"Everything is excellent, Ms. Matta... You have my word... And, nobody has contacted me about anything." Omar shook his head with every word. "And, would you be taking over Pedro's accounts too?"

The last statement was a little alarming to Bonita. She never knew Pedro had something separate from her father. But, she answered, "Si ", despite the fact that she didn't know what these accounts could be. They always shared everything, and kept the account under the family's parent company.

"Okay, so that..." Bonita couldn't finish the sentence because a bunch of movement outside of the window caught her attention.

Paris stormed into the back. "They're not with us then pointed to the five metallic G-Wagons. They were the G65 AMG edition; a slightly longer and more powerful version then their little cousin the G63 that most celebrities and entertainers drove in the States.

Hector spat through his sleeve and ordered the team to spread out and wait on his order to fire. They wanted to box the luxury vehicles in the hanger.

The SUV's came to a halt. Then the backdoor of the second vehicle opened. A tanned man with long curly black hair, mixed with strings of grey, stepped out smiling.

"Okay... Okay... Okay... Let's take it easy now." He said before closing the door behind him.

"What's your business here?" Hector yelled while standing next to the Sonoma steps.

"I just came to talk to Bonita."

All of the commotion had Omar startled. He couldn't believe that he was in the middle of such a dangerous event. Omar was a lawyer. A lawyer who dealt with creating shell companies for the wealthy and able. Not a thug or gangster or drug dealer as these people were. Violence wasn't a part of his repertoire.

"Paris, bring Sebastian to me."

Paris strutted to the door of the jet. She opened it up and waved Sebastian over to the jet.

Hector kept a close eye on the trendy guy. Sebastian was sharp. He looked like he came right off the pages of *GQ*.

Sebastian Gonzalez was garbed in a black Chanel suit, slim fit, with a white cotton short underneath of it. His silky black hair came to the shoulders, and he wore a neat one inch trimmed beard.

Sebastian appeared to be in his fifties but it was the appearance of a young fifty year old. It might have been because of all the money he accumulated through the years or maybe because of the stress free life he had.

The man was of Venezuelan decent but travelled extensively throughout the world on behalf of his employer.

Sebastian made it upon the jet. While stepping past Paris, he gave the Caucasian woman a wink and a nod of approval. The blond had a tiny mini-skirt on and she wore it well. The Balmain skirt showed every angle of the slim and toned frame. Paris was the very type of woman that he chased on a daily basis.

"Bonita... Bonita. Mamma sita. Why the alarmed face? I'm only here as a courtesy." Sebastian said, as he helped himself in to Paris' seat. "How are you today, Mr. Mossack?"

Omar gave a head nod and sat back on the sectional. He didn't understand why his presence was still needed at this moment. But the atmosphere was to tense to ask a question. Omar didn't want to interrupt the moment.

Bonita eyed Sebastian like a hawk. He had just confirmed her suspicious. They were making their move. It wasn't a question, now that the agency made the call and ordered the murders.

"Why the sudden visit?"

"The same offer that was given to your family. The silver or the bullet! We want twenty percent on all the shipments going to America, Canada and Europe. But, think first beautiful before you speak... This offer is on the table for a month." He replied not waiting for any small talk.

She couldn't reply. Bonita's body tensed up with anger. *How dare these people come and try to pull a hostile takeover by killing my family.* Bonita thought to herself. First, it would be the points on the shipment. Next, the permission to access the Port and shipping routes. And third, completely taking over the entire network. Bonita wouldn't allow it, at least not on her watch.

"Beautiful... Don't make this hard on yourself... You have a nice family in America. You're doing fairly well. Don't let the greed be the cause of all of that vanishing before your pretty eyes. Take the silver my love, as our Mexican friends would say."

Bonita was furious. *How could Sebastian sit there and speak so boldly of ruining her family's lives.* It was a rhetorical statement to herself. Bonita knew who Sebastian was and what he represented. She'd heard the rumors about how he was arrested in the early 90's for carrying out murders while he was an agent for Venezuela's secret police. After bribing an official, Sebastian was released from prison in January of 2000. Sebastian stayed there arranging deals for shipments of cocaine to be brought in to America, whichever way he could get them to the great Country's doorstep. It didn't matter. The agency just wanted it in. He was successful in this endeavor. Sebastian was living proof that crime does pay. They allowed him to start several shell companies that dealt with importing and exporting goods to America.

Sebastian's stint with the CIA didn't stop there. Later, he went back to his old ways, and the agency had him overseeing high-profile hits. The agency needed assets like Sebastian. They didn't want to get their hands dirty or end up in another scandal like the Iran-Contra incident.

It was well known that the agency was the cause for all the drugs being brought into America. Bonita understood this part, and knew that her father dealt with them to a certain extent. It was impossible not to. You had to wet their beak a little in order to get the drugs into the Country.

The CIA had close to a 70 year run at supplying drugs to America and abroad. They were in the similar vein as Pontius Pilate. The CIA washed their hands of the human tragedies, and the corruption of government offices.

It all started back in 1947 when a Wall Street lawyer and banker wrote, The National Security Act. The act called for the creation of a central intelligence agency, a group that could produce data and information around the world, so that America could be safe from threats and acts of terrorism. But they needed a lot of funding to do this. That's when they got into the drug and mercenary business. This is when a man named Clark Clifford brought the CIA backed drug bank called, BCCI into the United States. The bank had a long run but in the summer of 1991 it got caught up in a money laundering investigation. They shut down the bank, briefly then moved it into several shell companies that men like Omar Moassack created.

Bonita knew this was a dangerous man; an asset, mercenary and a collaborator for all types of suspicious people. The combination of such evil spelled out nothing but the word 'LUCIFER' across his bright face.

"I'll be in touch," was all Bonita replied with. She was still sitting and not willing to show an ounce of fear or concern for the dangerous man. Deep down, inside of her heart, Bonita wanted to kill him right then and there just to avenge her father's death. But, it was too dangerous at this point. She needed time and luck on her side because the CIA was a whole different animal to have as an enemy.

Sebastian stood up then buttoned up his suit jacket. "I hope it'll be sooner than later." He said, with the bright smile wiped off of his face. "Take care, Mr. Mossack." Sebastian gave Omar a wink before turning to exit the jet.

Destiny

Chapter 7

A large crowd formed a circle around the teenager standing in the middle of two abandoned homes. He wore baggie denim jeans and an oversized white t-shirt with a navy blue Atlanta Braves fitted hat to the back.

The small street was filled with cars and trucks that blocked any traffic trying to move through the tiny side street of this dangerous neighborhood. Most of them were squatters, as the cars and trucks were called by the locals who used and abused the vehicles for all types of purposes. But, they were used mostly to transport drugs and to commit robberies and murders in.

The traffic back up wasn't unusual for this street. It was a known drug strip, where numerous bodies had dropped over the years, and a place where you could find a nice dice game on any giving hour of the day.

Drug dealers, junkies, hoes, gangsters, and stick-up boys flocked to the scene. It was no different this day. The dice game had been in full swing, as the short kid named EC shook the dice hard in his right hand while glancing around the crowd. "Yo, bitch this for you... I want a dick suck and a bag on you." He stated with a smile. The high-yellow teenager was filling himself. The spot light was on him today because of his wicked shot. EC was hitting number after number, and he was up a few thousand. It was nothing major to most of the players standing around but just the thought of having this type of hood status of being the bul who had a gun game, and have a good shot on the dice had his adrenaline and confidence on blast.

"Nigga! I'll even give you a shot of this pussy, if you make this last point." The slimy with micro braids replied. She had been standing to his right with a hand full of twenties and fifties. All of her winnings came from EC's wicked shot.

The crowd roared when she stated that she would have sex with him, if he rolled the next number. It wasn't nothing unusual though because she was the neighborhood hoe.

EC grabbed his crotch by the statement. The thought of tearing the tall, well-developed, girl out of the frame had him focused. Even though, he had already hit her before. She was a freak and he wanted seconds. He then shook the dice real hard before throwing them against the wall.

All eyes were on the dice. It seemed like the world had stopped for a second, but it didn't. The dice bounced off the wall then hit the wad of money scattered on the ground. They stopped before hitting EC's white Airforce 1's.

"Click, clack!" Was all that could be heard because of the crowds focus on the dice. Everybody glanced up from the dice to see who was playing with their gun.

Two boys wearing cut-out white t-shirts around their heads, black t-shirts and denim jeans were running up to the crowd with their huge guns drawn. They had snuck up on the game from the alleyway that sat right on the side of the abandon home.

E.C. couldn't believe it. Two boys were trying to stick the dice game up in his neighborhood. Not the Highland Gardens aka Killa Hill! This was the ultimate smack in the face for him. A crime that carried the death penalty for any and all of participates in such a vicious act. He wanted to know who these two boys were that had ran up on him, looking like the Klu Klux Klan, and that was bold enough to rob him.

A lot of people spun off running in opposite directions. They were trying to get away from the boys. It was the common law of survival in the hood. When a gun was pulled out, and the person had a mask on, you ran. And, you ran for your life no matter what.

EC, and the tall redbone froze. It was them, and a few others that got caught slipping like a deer caught in the headlights. They couldn't make a move without the boys gunning them down. And, from the looks of it, that's exactly what they were prepared to do.

Tens, twenties, fifties, and a few hundreds were splashed across the ground. But, all eyes were on the robbers. "Yo, yo, put y'all fucking hands up! We ain't playing no fucking games." One of the boys said, heading towards EC's direction. He held a black Tec-9 with air holes on the muffler. A round clip curled a little bit out of the gun. The teenager waved it back and forth around the crowd. He was letting them know that he meant business.

The other boy who had a chrome .357, that had a long barrel, dashed over and started snatching the money off the ground.

"Cut! Cut!" Jamal said, yelling through a bull-horn.

He sat across the street in a black chair. Jamal wore a black and white Gucci bucket hat, denim jeans and black t-shirt that had 'Black Society' written on the front of it. The African-American director who had a handful of urban hits wasn't happy with the scene. It felt authentic but it seemed like it needed a little bit more. But he couldn't put his finger on it. Jamal turned around to ask Tate a question.

"Is this scene accurate enough? We need that true American touch to it... It has to flow, and have true-to-life touch to it."

Jay, Tate and a few of the young hitters from the Highland Gardens were standing inside of a yard. They were underneath a tree and watching a remake of an incident that happened in the late 90s.

"All of it except for the part of niggas running away and not upping on them... Yeah, niggas is going to run at the site of the stick-up buls but they going to run and grab they jawns... But, fuck all that... We need the actor who's portraying my man, EC, to go for his gun when they take their eyes off of him because that's what EC would do." Tate replied.

"Okay, we'll take a lunch break and repeat this scene from the top."

He yelled into the bull-horn to the crew, and everybody else that was involved in making the documentary.

At the sound of Jamal's instructions, the production crew and security started gathering everything up. The cars and trucks were moved out of the street and most of the crew were heading to the row house where a couple long picnic tables with food spread across them were sitting in the front yard.

Tate and Jay stood in the yard talking to their young hitters who they hired to make sure the place was secured. They didn't need it safe for themselves but for Jamal, and his production crew.

A buzzing sound went off and Jay grabbed the phone out his denim jeans. He glanced at the text, and stated that, "Aye Tate, the jawn spinning the block any minute."

"Who, the Miami jawn?"

"Yeah."

No less than a few seconds later an all black, tinted up, Mercedes Sprinter luxury coach spun around the corner on the 2600 block of Nolan Street then headed around to the bottom of Swartz Street where all the action was taking place.

"Aye Hak, go secure that alleyway for me, and make sure y'all on point out here... It's packed out this jawn... Keep an eye on the bul, and his crew while we holla at the broad."

The young savage didn't say a word. They went straight to their positions, and let the Old Heads run the show.

This had been the relationship of the young hitters, and the brothers since the night that they walked up in the abandon house and took Destiny out of it alive. The next day, after the incident, a meeting was called up the Gardens, in front of the SA's store named Peralta Food Market. Hak, Meer, Idris, Muscle, Tyson, Womp, and a bunch of other young hitters and dealers from around the Gardens were there.

Everybody had a voice, and a vote. The brothers were trying to unite the neighborhood, and bring it back to its glory days before the Feds had torn it apart.

The brothers broke down the plan of letting them keep the neighborhood because it was useless to fight over. Even though, the youngsters rightfully owned it now. They broke down that fighting over it didn't work out before when they had run most of the other Old Heads out of the neighborhood. So, with them keeping the hood, the brothers just wanted them to sell all their drugs, and hold them down when they needed hitters. They agreed to the plan. Hak's team, the Garden Boy Savages, would be the brothers, personal, hitters and Womp, Muscle, Tyson and the others would push all the work.

The brothers understood the consequences of such a move but it needed to be done. With, Destiny promising them at least 200 kilos a month they needed a face to push the product through the City and other spots around the Tri-state. They couldn't trust nobody else except the Killa Hill boys.

The luxury coach came to a complete stop in front of the corner house. Tate and Jay were standing in the yard by themselves, and talking about the documentary.

Destiny strutted around the front of the coach. She appeared sexy, even while she tried to dress down for the occasion. Destiny had a black, fitting, t-shirt, with 'Black Society' written in white on the front, that stopped right above her navel. She had a pair of black designer jeans on with a pair of throwback Manilo Blac tan knee-high boots, Destiny hair was down, and she started beaming when she seen the brothers.

A husky, bald head, black dude rounded the Mercedes behind Destiny. He had on all black, from the shirt to the boots, with a menacing grin on his face. The grin told you that he meant business but the lack of a weapon bulging from his hip showed you he lacked the intelligence for the job.

This wasn't an area or city where the buff, husky or juiced up bodyguards ruled, especially, the ones who didn't carry a firearm. He didn't know it but Hak already had the drop on him, just in case this wasn't a friendly visit from Destiny.

"How my boys doing?" Destiny said, stepping up to the brothers.

The lovely and friendly girl had wiped the ruff grill off their faces. Now, both of them had approachable grins on their faces. This was their girl.

The brothers had grown a likin' to the alluring woman from Miami who had the world within her grasp. They understood the connections she brought, and the level that they could obtain if they played it smart and fair with the woman.

Destiny was in a position to make them multi-millionaires, in the span of a year, and they both wanted and needed that. They hadn't been out of prison for two years yet. The stale and bland prison food, institutional lock downs, stabbings, black and white porn sheets, and racist correctional officers were still fresh in their minds. The brothers wanted to get rid of all these, inhuman, images of prison life, and live the life that they were destined to live like, as bosses. They had put too much work in since kids not too. This was their last goals or things to do on their bucket list. And, it was to get rich. Not hood rich but filthy rich.

Destiny opened her arms and went to Tate first. She gave him a big hug and kiss on the cheek. Then, went and did the same to his brother, Jay. "I told y'all I was coming to see the action."

"Yeah, I thought you were playing... I'm glad you came out. This documentary jawn going to be major," Tate replied.

"I hope so because I'm putting my name on it... Now, you know it got to be the shit for me to do that... Where Jamal at?"

"He over there eating." Jay stated while pointing to where most of the film crew were eating at.

Destiny turned to see the man and caught her bodyguard stepping up. "Brucie, I'm good... You can go sit in the coach... They got me protected out here."

"Dee you sure? Its crowded out here."

"I'm positive... My boys got me." She said then waved him off to the vehicle.

Bruce turned and stepped away but instead of getting into the coach he stopped then stood in front of the side door entrance.

"How's everything going? We been waiting for a few months on this work, you promised... My youngbuls is starting to press us to get them some shit... How long you think it's going to be before you get your hands on something?" Jay asked. He was ready to move the drugs. Sitting around and producing the film was cool but it wasn't like drug money.

"Soon... Soon... I'm waiting too... But, we got to be patience because when it starts moving this leisure time here is going to be over... But, in the mean time, make a great product."

"Oh, this film look like it's going to be straight," Tate said.

"Are y'all going to tell your stories in it?"

"Nah!" They both said, at the same time.

"Why?" Destiny asked. She was curious why they didn't want to tell their story about the Boyle Street Boys.

"We still got two soliders in the box, and we don't want nothing interfering with them getting out of prison."

"Oh, okay I see now but do you think that 'Chester Exposed' could be told properly in this documentary without the circumstances surrounding y'all release from prison? I mean that was how we got it green lighted."

Destiny knew the answer before even asking it. She just wanted to see where the brothers mind frames were at, and whether they had the ability to think outside of the box. Destiny needed them to be thinkers, and not just goons. Although, she needed both but in order to pull off the move that she had planned for them, and to uphold her part of the elite group, Destiny needed the brothers to be masters of the game.

"Don't worry about it... We got it... Everything gon be straight," Tate replied.

Destiny just stared at him. She believed the handsome man. She had too. Destiny had already funded the project for them. Even though, they didn't know it. She did it for a reason though. She already made the decision that she was going to make them rich. Their trust, loyalty and bravery for her determined this decision.

Destiny's main concern for them was being sent back to prison. They didn't deserve it, and she wasn't going to let that happen. So, Destiny secretly made a few moves, and got them an entertainment company up and running. This was a front she had made up for them strictly to keep the Feds off their lines.

The three had been dining out one day and Destiny pitched the ideal to them. Although, the brothers didn't want to do it at first, they accepted, eventually, because Destiny still didn't have the kilos yet.

Destiny then scrambled up some start-up money and got everything together on the legal side then placed the entertainment company in their names. It was their first legit business since being released. BLACK SOCIETY was born.

They needed this front just as bad as Destiny needed it. The Attorney General's Office, ATF, DEA and FBI would surely be working day and night trying to place them back in hell. Destiny didn't want that for the gangstas. She had other uses for them that involved getting money and living the high-life like her.

The brothers started the company 'Black Society', and decided on a project that turned out to be a documentary about their city. They called the story, Chester Exposed because that's what they were doing, exposing Chester for what it was worth. A cold-hearted, money getting city that bred everything from Drug Lords, Coke Starz to professional basketball and football players to murderers and hoes. They didn't plan on leaving out the snitches that ruined a lot of the official gangsters' lives.

The brothers had planned on placing all of that in front of the public's eyes, and let them decipher the situation of these cruel circumstances of people lives.

"I'm going to follow y'all lead on this one... I really don't know to much about writing a story but if y'all need a pretty model to make an appearance, I'm all game... I won't charge my normal appearance fee." Destiny said, and placed her hands on her hips and smiled.

"Naw, shorty this going to be a gritty tale. We don't need no supermodels in it... Ain't no supermodels come out of the city just yet, but you see my daughter over there." She gazed over to the crowd. "The bad one with micro braids... Her name is I'jon... She wants to be an actress and model. I need you to give her a few pointers and game about the whole process."

"I gotcha ya... Anyway, I wanted y'all to meet somebody. He sitting in the coach waiting on me... Come on, walk over there with me." Destiny said, before turning and heading to the vehicle.

Brucie was still standing there guarding the entrance door. He saw Destiny approaching and went to open up the side door. The brothers were directly on her heels, as she climbed into the spacious coach.

The inside of the luxury coach was immaculate and huge. It had all the amenities of a private jet with the tools of a mobile office. This particular one had a high-tech entertainment system that included iPads, internet service, a flat screen TV, and a full bed in the rear.

Destiny headed to the back and sat next to a light skinned bearded man. He looked like money, and it wasn't new money. It was that old, blue blood-dirty, drug money that he displayed from his style of dress and aura.

He sat back on the cushioned seats with his right leg slung over top of his left one. Balenciaga in orange letters spread across the bottom of his designer sneakers. The sneakers were made of orange leather, and the soles were white. Which matched the white jeans and white shirt that had thick designed strips of red, pink, orange and purple on it. He had a few smaller gold chains on but a thick gold, with diamond encrusted, Cuban link sat on top of his Hermes t-shirt.

Jay seen the goon first. He went and took a seat by the window. Tate followed and sat in the seat across from his brother. Both of them just eyed the man. They knew who he was but not personally. The brothers had just heard about the bejeweled and dangerous man.

Brucie slammed the door shut behind Tate and stood guard outside the vehicle while they talked inside. "Hold on now... I told y'all that this was going to happen... Bam close the partition for me..." Destiny told the driver, as she seen the aggressive stand-off by the men.

Destiny wanted this to work. She needed the team to be on one accord. So, this meeting between the gangsters was inevitable. It had to happen.

"Yo, we don't have any beef with dude." Tate replied trying to smooth the situation out.

"Y'all, fuck wit the bul Lil Nigga?" The man spoke for the first time. He needed to know the answer. It was important to him. He had already told Destiny that this would be the ice-breaker because if they were down with the Young Gunz then all bets were off. He didn't want to work with them. Destiny would have to than get her hands dirty.

"Look man, yeah we know the bul Lil Nigga... We watched him grow up. And, we fuck wit him and his peoples but did we have anything to do with the shit they were putting down in the streets? No!.. We were up in somebody's mountains bidding when they were running around getting money and dropping shit... Them niggas is gone... Most of them got elbows or dead. Major, look bru, we ain't got nothing to do wit that shit... About any drama or issues you got wit them."

"What about them BAM niggas?"

"Man, fuck them! We, on they line... Yeah, we heard about the incident wit ya sis down NC."

Major sat back and took in the whole conversation. *Were they telling the truth or trying to line him up too? Could these killers be trusted?* Intuition was a mutha fucka. He hated the fact that they were from the Highland Gardens. Major owed the neighborhood one but these two weren't the ones.

The brothers were right. They had been in a United States Penitentiary when Lil Nigga and his crew, the Young Gunz, terrorized the City.

The Young Gunz had rendered mayhem up and down the Tri-state area. And, one of those acts of violence was perpetrated on a man named Hanif.

Hanif was a hitter from the mean streets of Southwest Philly who had been locked up with Lil Nigga. The two had got close and Hanif turned Lil Nigga onto his favorite cousin, Wahida.

Lil Nigga and Wahida had a nice relationship until one day it all fell apart. The Feds were busting doors down and Wahida got shook. She spaced out on Lil Nigga and threatened to leave him. He didn't like her attitude and shaky demeanor. Lil Nigga felt she was a potential threat; a rat. He didn't need that in his life because the life he lived, he played for keeps. So, with the Feds getting close and snatching up a few of his partners and family, Lil Nigga had to leave her or else he would have to kill her in the long run. He had too much love for her to turn around and kill her, so he had to move on without her.

Lil Nigga stopped dealing with Wahida. She didn't take it too lightly. So, when he left one day she went and broke into his safe and stole almost a quarter-million.

Upon realizing who stole the money, Lil Nigga got even and his brother killed Wahida outside of a gas station in West Philly.

Hanif wasn't going for it. He felt obligated to revenge her death. Hanif tried on numerous occasions to kill Lil Nigga but they all failed. Lil Nigga didn't though. Lil Nigga caught Hanif on a side street in Philly.

Hanif was sitting in a brand new Benz with a female. Lil Nigga, and one of his brothers ran down on Hanif then unloaded on the car. Hanif was slumped within seconds.

Major knew the story and that Lil Nigga was behind the assassination. Nobody else had the heart to pull such a move on the click. Everybody in Philly knew that Hanif was on Major's team. The team that had the City of Brotherly love in a headlock, at the time. Plus, Hanif had been filling Major in on the run-ins that he had with Lil Nigga and on the fact that he was the one who killed their baby cousin, Wahida.

Major hated them Chester boys. He wanted them dead. But, his wish couldn't or wouldn't come true. Lil Nigga got locked up on RICO charges, and for the killing of a federal agent. He was done, at the moment.

"Okay, now, everything good?" Destiny asked staring at Major. She needed his approval or else it wouldn't work. Destiny trusted his judgment and street skills.

"We good!" Major said then extended his hand to shake on it with the brothers.

They accepted the offer, and the truce was official.

"But, one condition..." Major stated while sitting back down on the leather seat. "I want them BAM niggas dead... You got to find them for me.. I gave my sister, my word that I was going to see them niggas."

The brothers stared at each other. It seemed like de ja vu.

The brothers had vowed in prison to never discuss the act of murder with anyone. For the simple reason that, they had been set-up before like that, and it cost them 15 years of suffering in hell.

"We'll think about it because we ain't dropping shit for nobody... That shit right there is dead!" Jay said, in a really frank tone.

They didn't trust Major, and why should they. Major was still on the run for the indictment that Polo and Priest fell on. It had been going six years but the Feds still wanted him.

Destiny seen the tension starting to build up again.

She knew the brothers didn't feel comfortable with the request, and she didn't either. Destiny had brought them in to move drugs. Not to kill any rivals.

"Look don't worry!... We're here to discuss business and make money. Not revenge old beefs... And, Major please don't take that as an insult, as to what I just said because I understand you want revenge for them shooting Reeka but now is not the time nor place for that discussion."

"You right sis... We'll discuss it later... I'm Gucci." Major said with a devilish smile.

A smile that didn't sit right with the brothers but they acted like they didn't catch it.

"Well, then let's discuss the basis on the operation and how to stay under the radar." Destiny began going into details of everybody's roles, and how it should move forward.

After ten minutes into the discussion, the brothers and Major relaxed a bit and took in everything that Destiny was trying to break down.

Chapter 8

An extra long sofa and a white leather recliner sat like pieces of driftwood on a tiny sand island while a huge glass table dominated the center of the living room.

The condo was chic and simple just like Destiny wanted it. She was a fan of simplicity and that didn't change with the new position she played in life.

Destiny was back home in her condo; the Manhattan hideout that her and Polo shared for a while in the past.

Full body length mirrors lined three-fourths of the walls, and a large window overlooking New York City sat in the back of the living room. Destiny sat in the white leather recliner barefooted with her legs curled up to the chin. She was dressed in a pair of black spandex pants and matching sports bra that had the iconic Nike sign splashed across the front.

Destiny looked around and realized that with all the traveling, due to modeling, she had failed to remodel the place. The atmosphere and decor still reminded her of Polo; a memory that she was constantly trying to erase from her mind.

She leaned over and picked up the iPhone lying on the glass table. The phone had gone off and alerted her that a text had been sent.

Polo Jones #72364-066: Sweetheart, pick up the phone. Why u ducking my calls?

"What?" Destiny didn't understand.... How the hell, could he be texting her. The Bureau of Prisons didn't allow for their federal inmates to correspondence by text. Right when that thought was running through Destiny's mind, the phone rang. She flicked through the phone then waited to see who it was on the caller ID. An odd number came up. Destiny answered on the fourth ring. "Hello," she said, with a curious tone.

"You have a prepaid call from federal inmate, Polo. You will not be charged for this call. To accept this call dial 5. To block any future calls press 7."

Destiny pressed five and remained silent. She didn't know what to say. Destiny despised Polo, and his brother Priest.

"What's up baby? I see you screening my calls. Shit... What's up with that? I thought me and you had a better understanding than that?"

"Polo, I'm just tired of the bull shit... I just want to be left alone by y'all. You and Priest have cost me so much grief. I'm just done with putting up with the bull crap."

"Destiny, it's me you're talking too... I'm the one who has always been there by your side... Team Destiny! Remember that? Remember when you ain't have shit! Remember when you didn't have a career? You were just a struggling model."

"Please, I was never a struggling model!" Destiny was upset by the last comment because it was true. She didn't have nothing before Polo came into her life. But, she wasn't about to admit it.

"Then, what was you!" Polo asked but Destiny couldn't respond. "I brought you into the family and gave you a lane to move in..."

"Thank you!" Destiny stated with a sarcastic tone.

"Damn, who is it?"

"Who? what?"

"Who, the nigga you fucking?"

"Polo don't speak to me like that... You know I've always been faithful. I've been a good girl... I never cheated."

"Well, what the fuck is up? Why, you acting all bougee on me... With this attitude, like I'm beneath you or something... You know who I am and what I am about... I always had and always will provide for you and others."

"Polo, please stop with all of this... I'm just done! Please, I just want to move on with my life."

"How you going to do that when we're in business together? We have to talk because of the mutual interest in the business."

Destiny was speechless because of the dilemma that she was in. Running the Jones Foundation was crucial. She was sorta like in a crossroads with the ideal of her taking the company and saying the hell with the Jones brothers. She had considered it on many occasions, especially after Priest made the stupid move of trying to get her murdered behind Polo's cooperation with the government.

"We'll deal with that when you come home." Destiny responded back trying to ease any concerns of betrayal on her part. She knew Polo was intelligent. He didn't make it to such an epic level of drug dealing, if he wasn't. Destiny figured Polo was trying to check her temperature by asking the question. She understood that he loved her but with Polo having 18 months left on his federal sentence, the money was Polo's main concerns. He didn't want her to run off with it.

"I heard what happened too... You know the Feds is small."

"I don't know what you're talkin about?" Destiny replied but knew damn well what Polo was alluding to. Gazing out of the window and she remembered the favor she asked Tate to handle for her. He tried, but somebody else beat Tate to the punch. And, by coincidence it had to be some thugs from Chester who handled the situation.

A twenty-foot, razor-sharp, barbed-wire gate surrounded what appeared to be a massive recreation yard. But in reality, it was the size of two professional football fields combined. There were six two-story buildings rested on both sides of the oval shaped yard, separated only by the gates.

The place wasn't like the old penitentiaries in the movies with the big forty-foot brick walls circling the whole prison. Those were the days of old. The federal government, or Bureau of Prisons, who held the custody of all the United States prisoners, had updated the appearance and standards of modern day prisons. Central air, semi-clean cells, and cable-ready televisions improved the quality of life just a little in these new prisons.

Now, instead of the brick wall acting as a barrier or hindrance to prevent the convicts from breaking out, buildings where the convicts slept made up for the forty foot wall. The housing units, executive offices, gym, education department, and psychology area acted as a safety net.

The buildings circled the yard and closed everything inside the place. Just like a small community that functioned as one unit.

The housing units, now, held fourteen hundred hardened criminals that were sentenced to various lengths of incarceration including lifers in this particular facility. Some were innocent but most were guilty as charged and deserved every bit of the time they received for the heinous acts they committed while in the real world. The place was a level 5 institution, and labeled by the Bureau of Prisons as one of the roughest, dangerous and most miserable designations that anybody could serve their time in. This label was attached due to the fact of the well-known gang culture, the knowledge of officers racism towards colored inmates, and its violent occupants roaming the walkways, housing units and recreation yard.

The facility was tucked away in Northern California, right outside of Fresno, in Merced County. Atwater United States Penitentiary or USP Atwater, as everybody called it, appeared secured from the numerous gates, guards, and towers but it was far from safe. Inmates and officers alike were liable to get assaulted or savagely murdered by anyone whether it was the guards in a display of cruelty or the convicts stomping the officers out for being disrespectful to them. The prison already had numerous homicides committed by the inmates, and one officer murdered in cold blood, stabbed over thirty times.

The memory and incident was still fresh in the heads of officers, as well as the convicts although it happened over four years ago. The officers were still out for revenge. The convicts owed them a body and they hadn't paid up, as of yet.

The sun stood slightly above the dusty recreation yard. It was high noon on a Sunday, in the middle of June. California's heat was scorching. The hot rays beamed down on the buildings causing waves of heat to rise from the roofs. Four Correctional Officers garbed in light blue short-sleeve shirts, black boots, and dark blue Dickie pants stood on the grass in front of the middle entrance. They sweated profusely but were not necessarily bothered by the heat or sweat. Dark sunglasses covered their alert eyes, as they scanned and monitored the inmates strolling inside the gates in a bunched up fashion.

The recreation yard had been separated and segregated, to an extent, into three different sections, all of equal size. The section closest to the main corridor was yard one. It was filled with partial grass and a small baseball field that also transformed into a football field depending on the season. Several benches or seats, that resembled those that would be found at any park in America, surrounded the field for spectators to watch any games that were going on at the time.

The middle section was separated by gates and was locked after every secured move. The blacks, for the most part, controlled this area. Handball courts, two basketball courts, and the main sixty-foot guard tower occupied this locale. All types of business transactions occurred in this yard right under the watchful eyes of the officers in the tower clutching assault rifles by their sides. If they only listened to the conversations of some convicts, they would hear anything from them trying to sell food, nude pictures to actual million dollar schemes being hatched for future illegal endeavors outside the walls of prison or even inside of the prison.

Convicts poured into the middle section, and most of the Mexicans and Whites headed through the gate into the last yard. It held a huge dirt field used for soccer or football, as the foreigners called it, a couple of table and chair sets for the poker gamblers to play at, and one basketball court. Where, the Southsiders (Surenaos) exercised at on a daily basis.

All three yards were spacious and could house five hundred inmates a piece, if need be, due to an emergency or what not.

The level 5 facility also used controlled movements throughout the day in order to monitor the convicts every waking move. By being labeled as America's most sophisticated, intelligent and violent individuals, controlling them through daily activities was a must. This particular function saved lives no doubt. At any given time, eight out of the ten men were carrying a prison-made knife, or banger as some called it.

So staying alert was a necessity because the place could explode in less than sixty seconds. The inmates and guards understood this, which was established by those who stomped these recreation yards. So when conducting the controlled movements officers sometimes randomly searched suspicious convicts for contraband

In less than five minutes, the once empty yard filled with mostly white t-shirts and gray shorts worn by the men. It didn't matter what race you were. This was the Bureau of Prisons standard colors. Despite the mandatory dress code, the light colors helped them stay cool… a little.

USP Atwater's recreation yard didn't provide any shade. There were no trees, bushes, or anything else that could stop the sun from blazing down on the yard and scorching the inmates.

A loud voice shot through the prison's intercom system. "The ten minute move is closed! The ten minute move is closed!"

A few stragglers ran down the sidewalk leading to the yard trying to make it inside the gated place. One of them was Fareed. Most of the convicts and officers knew him well.

The lanky six-footer moved quick and with determination as if he had something of importance on his mind. Fareed pulled his white baseball cap down tightly above his eyebrows concealing his forehead and just revealing his menacing brown eyes. He was trying to keep the scorching rays from baking his bald head, but mainly his eyes. The tiny brim on the hat wasn't doing any justice. The rays were slightly baking his eyes and partially blinding him. This made Fareed twist up his face. He headed over to the back gate of the second yard where a couple of his men were posted against the fence.

They had been waiting on him. Most of them were from Philly except for Mar and himself of course. They were from the outskirts of Philadelphia in a city called Chester. It was only six of them in Atwater but they stuck together like a tight knit clan that had known each other for years. This sense of camaraderie and companionship amongst the group came about from their familiarity with each other.

The federal system had molded this characteristic into their prisoners, almost by force. The Bureau of Prisons mandated that you hung around your homies or car, as they called it. Which meant that if you were from Pennsylvania or Philly, then that's who you sat with when it was time to eat, who you walked the yard with, and occupied a cell with on the housing units.

The system approved of this type of segregated behavior especially the violent ones who couldn't comprehend nothing else but peace through aggression. So, by letting the homies, or cars, deal with their own and politic out conflicts with other cars that arose from the daily grind, the Bureau of Prisons took a hands-off approach. They understood that in order for a facility to run violence or riot free, the convicts had to have some leeway or say so about their own. It was the only proven way.

Fareed approached the group. He greeted Mar first with a closed fist and dapped him up. Mar was Fareed's celly and co-defendant. Both were serving 180 month sentences for Hobbs Act violations. They had 60 months in on the sentence, and both had given up on appealing their convictions any further.

Fareed and Mar had lost hope in the judicial system. It was rigged they thought. They had filed motion after motion, and appeal after appeal over the years and all were denied for various procedural or frivolous reasons. Now, their main concern was making it out of federal prison alive, and with some real money. The two had transferred from litigious motion filers to movers and shakers inside the penitentiary. Heroin was their only concern now. Who had it, who needed it, and how much it was going for were the only issues that they were worried about. This attitude came from their natural street competitiveness and lust for fame and wealth and no matter what they had to do in order to achieve those goals.

In Chester, they were home invaders who snatched money and drugs from hustlers or dealers, as some called them. Therefore, when the system refused to grant them an early release, they reverted back to what they knew how to do best. Take money by all means.

"Where you been at?" asked Mar. He was the shortest out of the group, and most laid back one. Mar wore a close cut and had some black Gucci sunglasses covering his tanned brown face.

"I had to run over on 3A to holla at da Mexican bul." Fareed responded as he continued to dap everybody else up.

"Who? The bul Mario?" asked a curious Omar.

"Yeah."

Mario Vega jointly controlled the Sinaloa Cartel. He operated out of Northern Mexico and had total distribution rights over the West Coast of America. But, Priest, who moved cocaine across Philly, was an exception to these rights. Priest father had worked for Mario before being killed in a drug deal, and was extremely loyal to Mario. When he was murdered, Mario took Priest under his care and taught him everything about the business. Priest prospered enormously from Mario's generosity and help.

But greed and a vision to exit the business intact clouded Priest common sense of loyalty. He schemed with another individual within the Cartel and set Mario up to be bumped out of the picture.

Priest cooperated with the government and testified against Mario in a federal drug conspiracy trial. Mario was found guilty based off of Priest's testimony and sentenced to a mandatory life sentence for running a Continuing Criminal Enterprise. Priest received a time-cut and was released from prison after doing two years.

On the very same day of his release, Mario's brother murdered Priest's wife and daughter. And, two years later Priest was back in federal custody being sentenced to a life sentence based off a racketeering conviction. His incarceration and sentence was based off the Sinaloa Cartel's reigning leader, Alex Diaz, and Priest's brother— Polo—cooperating with the government against him. Priest was then shipped to USP Atwater, in order to serve his life sentence. By Priest being released from custody after cooperating against Mario, his separation order was lifted from the Bureau of Prisons files.

The two, now, could be reunited in the same institution. Priest arrived at the prison during the night, right before the facility locked down. Fareed, Mar and Omar met Priest first. As was standard procedure in Atwater, Priest had been placed in a PA cell with Omar. That night Omar laid the law down to Priest, as it was once given to him by the seasoned convicts. Priest was new in the system and he needed to understand the culture and politics of the Bureau of Prisons. The Philly boys had heard stories about Priest case but didn't know him personally. They all knew his younger brother, Chance, who had got murdered prior to being indicted with Priest.

The next day at breakfast, Priest was introduced to everybody else from PA and they all planned to meet up on the yard. Mar, Fareed, Omar and Priest were talking while heading to the recreation yard. Fareed and Omar noticed Ty and Salaam talking to Mario like there was tension in the air.

All of the Pasias were on the yard and grouped up around Mario prepared for battle. He had acted as their leader or shot-caller. By him being from Mexico, Mario was considered a border brother, or Pasia, to the other Mexicans and he made all the decisions regarding them.

Fareed, Omar and Mar stormed straight over to the crowd but Priest froze up upon seeing Mario in the mob. All were strapped with bangers. The others didn't peep Priest's actions. They were too concerned about what was going on with Ty and Salaam. Nobody had a reason to concern themselves with Priest actions other the fact that he wasn't cut for this type of environment.

Omar and the others had assumed Priest stood up on his case and that he wasn't a stool pigeon. The three came within striking distance of the Pasias. Courage, determination and loyalty was engrained in their hearts and it showed in their demeanor that they were really ready to die, if need be, defending one another. Mario could care less about their zeal for each other. He wanted revenge and planned on tearing the yard up getting it. Mario was a man of sound mind, though. A thinker by far.

All the blacks, inside the second yard, picked up on the vibe. Some played the gates, while others stepped over and stood behind Ty and them. The blacks weren't backing down or showing any weakness amongst the pack. Mario seen the yard shift quickly and separated on racial lines. All the blacks were on one side and all the Spanish and Whites on the other. His heart and soul was still bent on revenge but he envisioned the damage that was about to occur. A lot of good men were on the verge of killing or being killed or seriously wounded behind a snitch. One of the lowest scums of the earth.

Mario contemplated fast and explained to Salaam about his dilemma. He had proof of Priest vicious betrayal; official court documents. Mario wasn't letting Priest slip away that easy. If anything, he was going to politic Priest an ass whipping.

The PA car understood Mario's complaint but couldn't let him do anything to Priest. It was a hands-off policy on the yard. Nobody could put their hands on anybody without first going to their homies or shot-

caller. PA didn't have a shot-caller. Nowhere in the system had they ever acknowledged that gang terminology. They decided issues collectively and democratically.

By Fareed and Mar being from Chester they didn't have the authority to lean on anybody from Philly. Even though they all moved as one, it was still politics inside the circle on that level, but they still had a voice and a vote at the table. The Philly guys had to make the call on who was going to deal with Priest. Salaam hung in West Philly, while Omar, Puff, and Ty were from North Philly and the decision fell on them. But Fareed was the best communicator out of the bunch, so he did all the talking with Mario for the group. Although he did guarantee Mario that Priest would be dealt with severely it wasn't negotiated on how he was going to be dealt with or what punishment he was going to receive.

Everybody shook on it and the groups dispersed, but not before Omar pulled Fareed to the side and asked him to lean on Priest. As the Pasias headed to the third yard and the blacks start strolling around the basketball courts, Fareed waved Priest over to the group. First, Fareed asked him whether or not he was indeed a stool pigeon for the government, although he knew the answer. He figured Mario wouldn't have went through all the motions or made up such an elaborate tale. Fareed still needed to see, if he was going to defend his honor. Priest answered in the negative and swore that he had proof about him not being a cooperating witness. Fareed felt disrespected and instead of just telling Priest to go check into the SHU, he snatched a flat-piece of steel, sharpen to the tip, out of his waist. He grabbed Priest with his left hand and yanked him close. Fareed slammed the banger in Priest's stomach. He slumped over, and screamed in pain. Fareed continued to ram the banger into his chest and head striking Priest every single time.

Mario didn't want it no other way. After hitting Priest several times, officers noticed the attack taking place and hit the emergency button. Fareed stopped the assault when the guards surrounded him and ordered for him to drop the weapon. He followed their request, but never laid down on the ground. He was cuffed and escorted to the

SHU. Priest survived the assault but was shipped to another institution.

"I bet you don't but just to let you know that shit affected me too."

"And! You know what you were getting yourself into... I tried to talk you out of it." Destiny hated the fact that Polo cooperated with the government. Just the thought had her disgusted. Destiny couldn't understand why she stood by his side this long.

"Damn, you just going to disrespect me like that?"

"You disrespected yourself Polo... You didn't care about me when you decided to help them... My life didn't matter to you... I almost got killed behind your mess, and frankly I hate you for that."

"Hate!"

"Polo, you know what I mean... I'm not going to lie about how I feel. My life was in danger behind YOUR act. So don't make this out to be like I'm the bad one... No, you brought this life to me... I didn't want this or deserve this."

The phone beeped one time indicating that it was a minute left to talk.

"I'm sorry sweetheart. I understand ya pain, and I promise I'm going to make it right with you."

"How?"

"You'll see... You'll see..."

"Yeah, yeah, yeah... I'll see, hun..."

"I'm serious, Destiny," This was all Polo could get out before the phone hung up in mid-sentence.

Destiny dropped the phone in the middle of her lap. She had to make a decision, and she had to make it quick. Polo had less than 18 months left on his sentence and he would come home and try to take his trust fund back from her.

The phone went off again and it snatched Destiny out of her daze. She picked it up and read the text.

Nas: I'm in Manhattan... Where are u at?

Diva: Relaxing in Philly

Nas: Philly? I thought u had to take care of some business in NY?

Diva: u stalking me!

Nas: nah just concerned

Diva: concerned bout what may I ask?

Nas: I'm just concerned that u might be hungry and I want to take u to lunch

Diva: is this business or pleasure, :)

Nas: a little bit of both, u can say. :) by yourself

Diva: yes

Nas: where?

Diva: let me pick u up

Nas: no

Diva: why?

Nas: because I said so, :)

Diva: excuse me... meet me at the W

Nas: u staying there

Diva: no, I have a few spots in NY but I just like the W

Nas: I'll be there at 2pm n I'll be waiting, :)

Diva: I'm sure u will be

Destiny responded before laying the phone back down between her legs. She smiled to herself because she knew Naseem had been trying to take her out for months and she finally decided the time was right to take him up on that offer.

Chapter 9

At the last minute, Destiny switched the plans up and opted to eat at the famed FRENCIE restaurant in the SoHo district of New York. She hated hotel food and wouldn't be able to sit through such a meal and not be aggravated by the thought. Naseem didn't mind and obliged to the ideal of having lunch curb side. He could care less where they eat because Destiny had been on his mind all month and he just wanted to spend some time with her.

It was a delightful day. The September weather was rather unique for the afternoon. There was a slight breeze but it was neither cold nor hot but a little in between of the two which made for a nice lunch date in the romantic city.

Destiny had arrived first. A young white male waiter sat her outside of the restaurant in a seat that overlooked the beautiful store fronts that ran along the iconic street.

She sat with her back to the entrance of the store alongside the huge window viewing the interior of FRENCIE.

Destiny placed her gold Jimmy Choo Cloud clutch on the ceramic table that had a stone pot with a small tree inside, and waited for Naseem to arrive.

Naseem strolled up looking dapper in a metallic black long sleeve polyester shirt and navy blue cotton suit by DSquared2 with a pair of black Canali shoes. He tapped Destiny on the left shoulder. She jumped a little bit.

"I'm sorry... I didn't mean to scare you."

"Boy, you didn't scare." She said smiling. "I was just thinking about something and you caught me in the middle of a thought."

"Was that thought about me?"

"No." She replied while standing and waving for Naseem to take a seat in front of her.

They both took a seat at the same time. "Hold up... I thought this was a business meeting because that remark doesn't sound like one."

"Well, I explained to you that it was a bit of both." Naseem couldn't help but say after staring the beautiful woman down.

"Okay than, let's get to the business first."

"Oh, straight to the point... I love an aggressive, take charge woman... By the way you look amazing today, as always." Naseem reflected on the statement and thought that using the adjective amazing was an understatement for her beauty. Destiny was more than amazing, she was stunning, elegant, chic or whatever else exotic or sensual word that you could use to describe such a fine woman.

Destiny tilted her head to the side at the statement.

It kinda caught her off guard but she was feeling the same way about Naseem. Although she tried to conceal the feeling because she had also started to taking a liken to Jay. Destiny didn't want to seem needy. But, she definitely seen some unique qualities in the man named, Naseem. The handsome brown-eyed man who seemed like he was down-to-earth and not one of those arrogant rich thugs.

"Thank you, you look handsome yourself."

"Did you order anything?"

"No, I just arrived five minutes before you."

Naseem gazed around the streets and inside the restaurant. "Oh, we're by ourselves today... Where's Brucie?" He said, with a little smile.

"I'm cool... I can take care of myself. I'm a big girl... What about yours, you come alone?" Destiny replied with a smile that Naseem could half-way see. The gold frame, aviator designed, Dior glasses covered the flirtation eye movement that Destiny did when she answered the question.

"I'm riding solo today... I had everybody stay back at the hotel because I wanted this lunch to be just us, too."

"Why is that?"

"Because, I wanted to have a lunch with a beautiful supermodel and not be distracted by hawking eyes of my detail."

"Ex-supermodel..." Destiny said with a sad heart.

"I'm sorry... Ex-supermodel... You know I been to some of those fashion shows that you appeared in."

"Boy, stop lying. You trying to psyche me up..."

"For real... I been to the one show that Tracy Reese threw... You were the face of her brand wasn't you?"

"Yup but that's my old life."

"I understand, you know by the life we chose, we sacrifice a lot to be in the position that we're in."

"I didn't choose this life it was sorta dropped into my lap... I loved my career. It took me to places that I never imagined that I would see as a little girl."

"You could have said no."

"No to what?"

"To joining us... I mean we didn't force you to join."

"Well, you didn't but I felt obligated to a certain person or people to make sure everything was going to continue on." Destiny replied with a heavy heart. She took the glasses off and placed them next to her clutch.

The waiter came out with two menus then placed them on the table. "Could I get you two any drinks before ordering?" He asked looking back and forth at them.

"You could get me a French Vodka with poppy syrup. Do you have that in stock?"

"Yes, sir, we have it... That's a special one not to many people order this cocktail."

"I'll just take a glass of water for starters."

He wrote down the requests and disappeared back into the restaurant.

"Okay, now where were we! I think I was telling you how sexy you look in that outfit."

Destiny blushed by the remark. She was lost for words. The outfit had been a last minute decision that she knew would appeal to Naseem.

"No, we weren't talking about that... I think we were getting around to speaking about the shipments coming in... My boys are begging for me to unload the material on them. I'm hearing the streets are pretty empty. We need to capitalize, quickly, on this." Destiny said, closing her vintage Donna Karen jean jacket that laid over the top of an orange and green Valentino Rhino printed dress that came to the middle of her shiny thighs and had a long split down the top part of the dress, which showed a lot of cleavage.

"Sorry... I mean they kept distracting me."

"The stunning green and gold beads or my little girls?"

"Both!" Naseem said with a smile then got straight to the point. "That's really what I came to talk to you about... Everything is in motion. Now, remember how we set it up. You're going to be in charge of the three ports on your side. Philly, Marcus Hook and Wilmington, Delaware... Manhattan is out of the question. It's to much of a hassle and I would only let my people take care of that because it's a lot more complicated than the rest. Now, as we talked about before, the shipment is coming through the Marcus Hook Port, the one right outside of Chester, on this run, so be prepared to move soon."

"Okay, I'll have my team on standby."

The waiter returned with water and the vodka. He placed them in front of the two then asked, "Would you like to order now?

"Yes, I would like the special of the day... I think it would be the scallops cooked with Jerusalem artichoke extract, and a chestnut-stuffed roast quail."

"Okay, and for you sir?"

"I never had that before. Is it good?"

"Excellent!" the waiter replied.

"I'll take the same."

The waiter dashed off into the restaurant.

"So, tell me about yourself Mr. Gordon, if it's okay with you... I mean you over there giving me all these compliments and stares like your undressing me with your mind or something... You have a wife?"

"No..." Naseem wasn't lying because technically he wasn't married to Bonita. Besides that, they had vowed to keep their relationship a secret for the time being. Too much was at stake.

"Any kids?"

"I have a little girl."

"Ah, ain't that sweet... I betcha she's a daddy's girl, too."

"Yup, I love my Bella... What about you?"

"Nope, what you see is what you get... I'm single, as you know, with no kids... My career was my only baby."

"Any secret lovers, in some distant place of the world... I know that career of yours took you too many cities, states and countries."

"No, I was a faithful girl at the time... I was waiting on the love of my life... My jailbird boyfriend, Polo. I didn't need nobody else. With him and my work, my life was complete."

"Well, I guess it's not anymore... I mean I don't mean to be so rude but I can see that your lonely and need a little bit of excitement in ya life."

Destiny just smiled at the thought. *How could you possibly bring any excitement to my life?* She thought to herself then stated, "So you think I'm lonely."

"Maybe... We're going to take care of it though... Don't worry about it."

The waiter brought back the food and they dug into the meal. Through bites of food and more drinks of the vodka, the two started to open up more.

Destiny couldn't believe it but she was falling for the charming man. Everything about Naseem was pulling her into that direction. She didn't understand why he was having such a powerful pull on her. Destiny had been around the world and seen some of the most polished men. Rich ones, handsome ones, charming ones and ones with drop-dead physiques, and even some with a mouth-piece that could make the most sophisticated woman come out of her expensive lingerie and let you dig her out right there in front of millions. Through all of this, Destiny maintained her composure around them. But, it seemed like she couldn't around Naseem. He was different.

They finished eating then discussed some more points of the business then Naseem asked her, "let me take you home?"

Destiny smiled at the question. She didn't know whether he meant to hers or his. She didn't care though. The juices were flowing and Destiny desperately needed her itch taking care of.

"Excuse me! I'm not that type of girl." She stated in a playful but flirtatious way. Destiny wanted to make him work for it. She wasn't going to give it up that easy. "How you know I didn't bring my own car?"

"You're a New Yorker... Nobody drives." Naseem said, and gave her that boyish smile.

"Well, I do drive but I took an Uber today... And, I'm not a New Yorker... I'm a Dade County girl."

"My bad... Now come on..."

"I didn't say I was coming with you." Destiny replied trying to be kinda feisty.

Naseem didn't bother to protest her statement. He knew she was playing hard to get, and he wasn't going for it. Naseem had been feeling the vibes and playing along with all the little flirty games she been tossing around.

He stood up then pulled out a small wad of money. Naseem placed four hundred bills on the tray. Destiny started gathering her things up off the table.

She stood up and got herself together before placing the glasses back on her face. Naseem grabbed her by the hand and escorted Destiny down the street.

Destiny didn't protest the move; she just went with the flow. She loved a man who took control of the situation and provided security to her. That's how she felt when Polo was around; fearless. Polo had provided

Destiny with every comfort and security that he could provide her with in the world.

Now, it seemed like Naseem was taking that route. He didn't mind and never took no for an answer, and that was from anybody. Naseem believed that, if there's a will, there's a way.

They bent the corner and hopped in to Naseem's SUV. He had lied to Destiny; sorta. Naseem had the driver park around the corner from Frencie's and waited for him.

The SUV took off into traffic and headed to Destiny's spot. They did a little sight-seeing, and drinking in the back before finally pulling up in her condo's garage.

Naseem didn't bother to ask. He got out of the SUV along with Destiny and they took the elevator up to her floor.

The whole ride was in silence. Nobody said a word. Destiny couldn't believe that she was actually taking Naseem up to her home. No man had every stepped foot in the place except Polo. Now, Naseem was just steps away from entering her palace.

They stepped off the elevator and headed towards Destiny's door. She was having second thoughts. *I can't do this. I don't even know him.*

Destiny reached in her clutch then grabbed the keys out. Her hands were slightly shaking. Naseem touched her hands, softly. "What's wrong?" He asked looking Destiny in the eyes.

She wanted to melt. The vodka started having its affects on her, and Destiny wanted Naseem so bad to take her in the condo and please her well.

"Nothing."

"What's wrong? Why are you shaking?"

"Naseem, how could I say this ... I haven't been with another man since I met Polo... And, that's been almost 6 or 7 years ago... This is new to me." Destiny said, before opening up the door and letting Naseem in.

He stepped into the place and stopped at the entrance. Destiny closed the door behind her and gazed at Naseem.

Naseem turned around and stared Destiny in the eyes. He wanted her, and he wanted it bad.

Destiny couldn't hold the gaze, so she dropped her head down. Naseem, gently, lifted her head up and the two locked their eyes once again.

She closed her eyes, and Naseem leaned forward and pecked her on the lips. Destiny didn't fight it. She welcomed it, and pulled his head closer and they started kissing in a passionate way.

Naseem caressed her and pulled Destiny closer. She couldn't take it no more. The juices were flowing and she wanted more than a tender touch of the hand.

Destiny pulled back from the kissing then grabbed Naseem by the hand. She led Naseem through the halls then into her room.

Naseem stopped at the bed. He gazed at Destiny then pulled her closer. Naseem started kissing and licking Destiny all over her lips, neck and ears. Then, he just suddenly stopped. "I can't do this to you... I feel like I'm taking advantage of your vulnerability."

"Take advantage of me than... I want you too... I want to be with you." Destiny said then started taking off her clothes.

Naseem shook his head, no. But, deep down he wanted to do it. "I can't... It just don't seem right to me."

Destiny was confused. It was usually her telling the man to stop at this point. Which was the truth because nobody had got pass this stage since Polo been gone.

"Destiny, you're special... Just like a rare jewel... And, from this day forward I'm going to treat you like it."

Destiny stood there with her perky breasts, brown nipples sticking out, andsee-through boy shorts type panties. It was a site to see, and Naseem loved every bit of it. But, she deserved better.

"This is what I'm going to do. Clear your schedule in two weeks and I got a surprise for you."

"What?" Destiny asked before she sat down on the bed. She grabbed the sheets and covered up.

"Don't worry about it. Just be ready when I call... We take care of this business first then we're going to have some getaway time." Naseem said, heading over to Destiny. He kissed her on the forehead then turned around and headed out of the door.

Destiny was speechless. She couldn't understand what had just happened. But, she realized that Naseem might just be the one.

Chapter 10

Gold and glass chandeliers hung from the high ceiling. Destiny strutted over to the twenty-foot glass windows that covered the whole living room side of the wall which included a double-door entrance to the Juliet style terrace that had oak and gold handles. The scene was mesmerizing. She viewed the harbor's edge in Kuwluon trying to spy down on the city of Hong Kong below. Light rays of the sun bounced off of her cream coffee color frame. Destiny stood there in the nude. Breasts still looking perky in her early 30's, love box still moist, but yet she felt scared and awful at the same time. Destiny couldn't believe that she had actually gave up the goodies to Naseem. But it felt good to her. She enjoyed it and melted with the slightest touch of Naseem.

After taking care of the business first, Naseem and Destiny snuck away from everybody. They had promised each other that it would be a secret. The two didn't want anybody in the group to find out that they were seeing each other. It was hard though. Especially for Destiny because it had been so long that she had been really into a man. They phone tagged and texted each other daily after the night Naseem left her in the room with a wet love box. By Naseem resisting the urge to take advantage of Destiny that night, it just made her want to pursue him even more.

Destiny was falling in love hard and quick. That was normal for her though because she was the long term relationship type. She had never been involved in the one-nighters or the random boy-toys. Destiny really was a good girl.

A waist-length gold telescope with oak legs stood in front of the glass window. Destiny stepped over then bended over to look out of it. The curiosity of viewing the city was just to appealing to her.

Naseem walked out of the hallway then stepped into the bright room.

This was the first time that he really paid attention to the details of the room. It was superb. It had a walnut and cream color scheme and touch-screen technology for lighting, music, and the televisions.

Destiny didn't notice or feel the presence of Naseem staring at her little bubble from behind. He was dressed in some black boxer-brief's that had LV in white going around the waist line with no shirt or socks on. Naseem rubbed through his, peach fuzz, chest and simply admired the beauty.

Destiny was a free-spirit and didn't have any shame of showing off her features. She didn't have a huge booty or breasts but they were normal and just right in all the places that mattered.

He crept over towards Destiny. The nice mounds hung.

She still didn't hear the steps on the fluffy carpet. Naseem got behind her then placed both hands on each side of her hips and eased up on Destiny. She didn't jump or break her train of thought.

"Have you ever seen this view? It's so amazing... I can't believe that I never been to this place before."

"Nah, this is my first time staying here. It was highly recommended to me by a friend." Naseem said then headed over to the glass doors.

He opened the glass doors and stepped on to the terrace. The would-be walls were also made of glass and small trees were strategically placed around the small area on the floor.

Naseem turned around and said, "Come here look at this view."

Destiny stood up and started to go before stopping at the doors. "What, if somebody sees me? I don't think we're the only ones with a telescope in our room."

Naseem just held his hand out. "Baby, this is the presidential suite... We're to far up for anybody to see you, and no I don't think everybody has that expensive telescope in their room... This is special here...

Special! Special for a special woman."

Destiny heart melted. She stepped out to the terrace and Naseem embraced her in his arms.

A small fog hung over top of the harbor with hills of a mountain to the side, but, the city down on the left side of the harbor could be seen. The view was extremely hard to see from their stand point.

"Naseem please tell me I'm not dreaming."

He leaned over and kissed her ear then licked around the edges before heading down to her neck. "It's not a dream... This is all real."

Destiny turned to stare Naseem straight in the eyes and said, "That's what I'm afraid of... It seems like you're just too good to be true."

They stared at each other without saying a word. Naseem was caught up in his thoughts. He wanted to tell Destiny so bad that he was engaged to Bonita and that they had a happy family and life. But, his conscious kept fighting him from doing.

"I mean you're successful, handsome and you know how to treat a woman... Why?"

Naseem broke the stare and gazed off into the hills.

He couldn't look Destiny in the face and continue to lie. He was growing feelings for her.

"Let's just soak this moment up... We got plenty of time to talk and discuss our future."

Destiny placed her head on his chest then closed her eyes. She knew it was too good to be true. *He has a woman and a family*. Destiny thought to herself.

They remained there cuddled for ten minutes before Destiny stepped off and went to get dress. The two had planned a big day. They were going shopping then to Quarry Bay to see a few exhibitions by some controversial artists which one in particular was Ai Weiwei then they scheduled to dine back at the Peninsula.

Naseem took a long shower washing away the aroma of love making. He felt bad for the position that he was placing Destiny in. Naseem was falling for her but he didn't want to leave Bonita. She was the perfect wifey type; loyal, rich, smart an excellent mother and drop-dead gorgeous. A man couldn't ask for more except maybe for Destiny. She had all of the same qualities more or less besides the baby and connections to the drug lords.

He stepped out of the shower then grabbed the terry cloth robe. Naseem walked through the small hallway back to the living room.

A buzzing sound kept going off. Naseem stopped then headed over to the knee-high glass table with three white chairs surrounding it then snatched the phone.

"Yeah."

"I'm sorry Mr. Gordon but you have a visitor that has to see you." Naseem bodyguard said who had been posted outside of the suite.

"Who is it?"

"Mr. Gonzalez... Mr. Sebastian Gonzalez."

Naseem couldn't believe it. He knew who Sebastian was and what he represented.

"Is he out there with you, and is he by himself?"

"Yes, he's here and with one guy."

"Okay, bring him in." Naseem replied and sat the phone on the table.

Sebastian strolled in through the door garbed low-key in a black business suit. He was followed by a 6 foot 3, buzz cut, slim white man who also wore a black suit. They headed through the living room and made a quick observation of the interior before reaching Naseem.

Naseem stood there with a robe on. Mark, his bodyguard, followed by the suited white man then stopped when they approached Naseem.

Naseem waved for Sebastian to sit in the chair. He accepted the offer then took a seat while buzz cut stood behind him.

Mark, the two hundred pound and professionally trained private security officer, stood behind Naseem.

"Why such the unannounced visit?" Naseem asked, curious of why this CIA backed operative would be visiting him in Hong Kong.

"Strictly business... You can understand that, right?"

"Of course..." Naseem replied with a confident tone.

"The money has slowed up in the States." Sebastian responded without breaking the stare. "And, I'm hearing that your group or whatever that its called, is the cause of it."

"Who told you this?"

"Well, it ain't who... I think the better question would be why... I mean, you know our friends doesn't take this type of insult lightly."

"So, what does that have to do with me?"

"It has a whole lot to do with you... Look, I'm not here to break your balls or anything... I've been sent with a simple message... Work for us or we might have to break up that cartel you're trying to form on American soil. I mean, have some damn respect."

Naseem couldn't believe it. They were trying to come in, and regulate the cocaine trade on the main land that had ceased to exist after Danilo "Chanchin" Blandon was arrested in 1996. Danilo was king at the time, and he supplied the South Central native called Freeway Rickey.

Damn, it's happening all over again and their trying to trap me off in it. Naseem remarked to himself.

"We know that Bonita Matta is taking over the family business and that's your daughter's mother, right?"

"Yes..."

"She now has full access to the Colombians, to the ports and to you... Look, we just want what's due to us."

"And what's due?" Naseem asked not denying the fact that if Sebastian info was accurate or not.

"Naseem let me tell you this... Bonita has been giving an option to help us to export the product to the States and other countries... But, the time line is getting short. We know that your a reasonable man who knows what it's like to grow up with nothing. She hasn't felt that a day in her life but she will and maybe a federal prison, if our terms aren't meant."

"What terms are those?"

"Let us deal with that but I ask that you two think long and hard about my offer... Everything in America would be promised to go through you, and this is on top of whatever Bonita or any other cartel is sending you... But, you got to convince her to come around and agree to our terms." Sebastian finished then stood up.

Naseem followed and just stared at the man. At that moment, he figured out why Pedro and Luis were murdered.

"You'll have full control of America's drug trade... You dictate the prices and purity. And, Naseem you got my word on that... We're going to make you the riches black man in America history and to show you that we mean business I'll even get them to release your brother, Titan...

"This is total access to do anything you please. You'll be above the law... Unprecedented for any black living in America."

Naseem was speechless. He couldn't believe that such an offer was presented to him of this magnitude.

"I'll be in touch. Next time we meet. I hope you're prepared to accept the offer." Sebastian said then stormed out of the room.

Destiny stood in the middle of the hallway wearing a black Prada strapless dress and red pumps. She clutched a red Chanel handbag in both hands. Destiny had caught the whole conversation. She was lost for words. Destiny couldn't believe that the devil was trying to make a deal with Naseem.

After they left, Naseem sat back down in the chair. He started rubbing his head. The offer was too good to be true. It had to come with some strings attached but he just couldn't put his finger on it.

Destiny stormed in to the living room. Naseem turned and stared at her. She start shaking her head. "No, Naseem! No, Naseem!"

"What?"

"You can't do this... Don't work with them. Please don't work with them."

Naseem got up then went to the glass windows. The night was falling.

"Baby, I seen firsthand what happens when you team up with them... Naseem, I'm telling you it's a set up..."

He turned to face Destiny. "I might not have a choice."

"You always got a choice. You always have a choice to do right or wrong. Nobody can take that from you."

"It's different with them Destiny... They're not the FBI or the DEA or the locals. These are the most corrupt, ruthless and dangerous people that is on this planet... They decide history over a cup of coffee. This is real baby."

Destiny moved over to the window by Naseem, so that she could look directly in his eyes. "I told you I didn't want to be a part of that... You promised me! You promised me!" Destiny said with tears running down her eyes. She dropped the clutch then started beating on Naseem's chest.

He placed her in a bear hug. She stopped swinging and was crying on his chest. "I'm going to take care of it... I'm going to take care of it... I'm going to take care it. Don't worry about it. I'm going to figure this out."

Destiny pushed Naseem away from her then stormed to the room. Naseem was lost for words.

He wanted to accept the offer. Titan would be released. He would become the richest black man in America with their help and he wouldn't have to a left a finger to get it. He could delegate all of the important aspects of the business out to the other partners. But, he had to cross Bonita to achieve this.

The phone started buzzing. Naseem headed over to the table then picked it up. A text came through:

Bonita: Where are you? We need to talk its important.

Naseem: Out of the country taking care of business. How's Bella doing?

Bonita: She's fine... When will you be back?

Naseem stared at the hallway before considering the question. He had planned to stay for a week in Hong Kong with Destiny but things weren't looking good for the home team.

Naseem started punching away:

Naseem: A week at least.

Bonita: No, I need to see you immediately... An old friend had come and gave me a visit a few weeks ago.

Naseem: Give me two days and I'll be in LA.

Bonita: Okay, I'm leaving today. I love you, Papi!

Naseem was shocked. Bonita had made her decision without him. He needed to get back to America, and soon.

Naseem leaped up from the chair and went to comfort Destiny because she badly needed it.

Destiny

Chapter 11

Bonita arrived at the couples Malibu home a week before Naseem got back to the States. She had planned, plotted and showed plenty of force and authority while in Panama. At the moment, there were no current threats from other ambitious cartels, families or crime organizations in the Central and South American regions to challenge the mighty Matta's.

She loved the thought of victory. But, she still had one Achilles heel that needed to be cured. And, that was Sebastian and the mighty Agency behind him. It was a hard one to fix especially when they wanted blood.

Bonita contemplated long and hard about how to handle the problem. She tried to think of all the things that her father would do or something he probably said, but nothing came to mind.

She sat in the spectacular living room with the two sliding oak doors wide open overlooking the infinity pool and impressive lawn. Bella ran back and forth with the nanny on the lawn blowing bubbles on the warm and sunny day.

Bonita took peaks at Bella whenever she heard the little girl laughing and having fun, as she sat on the creme sofa. She had the laptop in front of her and started typing away.

She paused then gazed around the huge room. The ceiling was an oval shape with a moon roof and colored white.

Naseem stepped into the room, as she had her head back looking at ceiling. He sat across from Bonita on the twin sofa.

"What's wrong? You look stressed."

"I am... I mean, what are we going to do? A decision has to be made either way."

"I agree... Maybe, we should deal with them for the time being until we find a better situation."

"I was thinking the same thing but I can't get over the fact he, indirectly said that they ordered the assassination of my father and uncle..." Bonita dropped her head down then rubbed both hands through her hair. "They or he will be held accountable for that... Somebody will Naseem... I couldn't see it no other way."

Naseem didn't comment on the subject of killing. It would be a dangerous move, he thought himself. Especially, during this shaky time. Revenge was best served when the enemy least expected. "We need to wait until we're strong enough for the revenge part... I mean, all signs of transgression would be pointed towards the Matta's and Bonita we can't take the CIA to war." He said then gave her a long stare to show how serious the matter would be if they attempted such a move.

"Well, we need to think of ways to counter such a threat, if they decided to move first." Bonita replied then gazed out to Bella.

Naseem understood the concern and he wanted to do the same. *"We have to out think them at their own game... What's their main weapon of war?"* He said, thinking out loud rather than a question posed.

"Information!" They both stated at the same time.

"We need to track down the biggest and baddest hackers in town." Bonita said, in a somber tone.

"No, not in town, in the world."

Bonita started tapping away on the computer. She wasn't on Google but she was trying to find info on where to find these people. Bonita started coming across stories of the biggest and most sophisticated hacks in history. She needed to get to the source. Bonita wanted to see who were taking credit for these invasions.

"We got to be careful because what if they are contractors and work for them."

She stopped in mid-stroke and peered up at Naseem. Bonita never thought of that angle. Then a revelation came down to her all at once. It was as if she were prophesying at the moment of clarity.

"We're going to Russia. I need Eric Snowden."

Naseem couldn't believe his ears. It would be a smart move, if Snowden wasn't viewed as a traitor to the United States. Getting involved with Snowden would be worst than getting involved with Sebastian. At least with Sebastian you were on America's good list.

He got up then moved over to the side of Bonita. Naseem sat down then wrapped his right arm around Bonita. She stopped typing then leaned back and accepted the warm embrace. Bonita needed it.

"We need to think this through a little bit more... I don't know about Snowden. I think that's like the worst person to be associated with since Bin Laden."

"You may be right but we have to win... I'm not letting them take my family legacy, our legacy for that matter... We will fight to the end."

Naseem understood her concerns. He didn't want to see the empire crumble either but they needed a different approach to the problem.

"I'm going to think of something." He stated then placed a kiss on her forehead.

Bonita closed her eyes. *All I need is a little time. I could pull this off.* She remarked to herself then opened her eyes. Bonita started rubbing up Naseem leg.

He had a white pair of Versace linen shorts on with nothing on underneath them. She rubbed further then found his love muscle. It

103

started to awake, as soon as she had commenced the rubbing of his thigh.

Bonita started, gently, stroking and rubbing Naseem's manhood. She peaked up and looked out towards the open doors.

Bella, and the nanny were seated at the end of the lawn staring out at the rolling hills of Malibu.

She then unbuttoned the shorts and pulled out the massive baby-maker. Bonita kissed it first then licked around it before taking a mouth full.

Bonita didn't go further than that. She held the baby-maker with one hand and worked on just the head. Bonita was sucking and slurping.

Naseem ran his hand through Bonita's hair, as he stretched his head back on the sofa.

"Ohh, I miss this..."

Bonita didn't respond. She just closed her eyes then took it in her mouth deeper and deeper. Bonita was enjoying it the same way Naseem was.

She opened her eyes then let up. Bonita peaked back at the entrance and the two were still in the same place. She took off her tiny white shorts and let them fall to the cream tile floor. Bonita sat on his lap from the back then closed her eyes.

"Ohh..." Was the sound she made upon sitting down on the stiff pipe. Bonita was loving it. They hadn't seen each other in months. And, this was the first chance they got to make up for the lost time. Bonita continued to bounce up and down. She didn't bother to see, if Bella or the nanny was watching. She was lost in ecstasy.

"Bzz... Bzz... Bzz..." A buzzing sound started going off from the phones and computers. Bonita didn't pay it no mind but Naseem leaned up and glanced around her.

"Hold up baby... Hold up!" Naseem tried to stop Bonita. She didn't pay him no mind. Bonita was in the process of cumming.

Naseem grabbed her by the waist and stopped her rhythm.

She then stared at the computer. The Google alert had went off then went straight to CNN news.

"Oh my God!" Bonita stated before rising up off of Naseem then grabbing her shorts. She hurried to put them on, as Naseem fixed himself up.

"Look at this!" Bonita pointed to the screen.

The headline read: Panama Papers. A picture of Omar Mossack's office in Panama City was splashed across the T.V., as an anchorwoman stood in front of the place breaking the news.

Naseem grabbed his phone, which had been going off too. He flicked through the emails. All of them were from Sebastian. He sent Naseem pictures of Destiny and him standing on the terrace in Hong Kong. Destiny was nude. There were pictures of him and Destiny in New York together, at the airport, and coming out of the Trump International.

He couldn't believe it. Sebastian was pulling all of the tricks and schemes out in order to get his goal accomplished.

Destiny shook Naseem back into existence with the next revelation. "They out'ed us! The bastards shamed us to the world... Look at this..." She said then pointed to the CNN's website that stated: An investigative journalist came across 11 million illegally hacked documents. These documents contain names, companies, and public officials who have previously undisclosed, offshore corporations around the world. This revelation is proof these people and corporations is, intently, abusing the financial legal structures.

'The documents has proof that the law firm has ties to the Russian and Syrian presidents, prime ministers and other financial play makers around the world.

'The investigation is still ongoing and may lead to criminal charges in the United States, and other sanctions by the Global Forum for Transparency and Exchange of Information for Tax Purposes Abroad.'

Bonita couldn't contain herself. She stopped reading the statement after viewing a footnote on the site that showed how the Matta family holdings were linked to the illegal drug trade. The report placed the Matta's family name alongside some of the known international criminals like Semion Mogilevich, a Russian mafia leader, and Diego Perez-Henao. Diego was the reigning leader of the Los Rastrojos. This organization was considered to be the largest supplier of drugs in Colombia.

It was frustrating for Bonita because Diego was her number one supplier. Diego controlled the main smuggling routes into Venezuela and Panama. And, he was madly in love with Bonita.

The direct link by her companies, and Diego's association with her could bring a lot of scrutiny to Bonita's exporting activities, which in turn, could stop the flow of cocaine reaching not just America but other countries as well.

Sebastian was playing his cards right. He knew that Diego wouldn't deal with him at all because of his legal woes with the United States. So it was a must that he pressed Bonita on letting the CIA wet their beak a little bit.

"They moved first, we have to negotiate." She said then stood to walk out of the room. Bonita couldn't believe it but then again she could.

This was their main play. Bonita knew there had to be more dirty laundry laying around that the CIA was holding back until the right moment.

Naseem laid his back on the couch. Sebastian was pushing forward with his agenda, and the pictures just topped it off. Naseem didn't want them to get out. He couldn't betray Bonita like that. Even though he had suspicions about her having an affair but couldn't prove it.

Bonita sat on the toilet with the phone in her hand. The news of Diego could ruin her. It could tarnish her business reputation and the relationships that came with it. She had to reach out to Diego in order to let him know that they had a problem, and a major threat to their cocaine business.

She quickly typed a text on the Blackberry that was used for him only.

Bonita: There's a huge problem.

Diego answered her text immediately.

Diego: how's me love? What's the issue?

Bonita: ours names have been linked together in the news.

Diego: I don't pay attention to American news, what are u talkin' 'bout?

Bonita: we were linked together on CNN about having secret offshore accounts that we have in order to hide the drug money.

Diego: me love don't worry, who has done this?

Bonita: Sebastian.

Diego: don't worry, I will take care of it.

Bonita: how soon?

Diego: in due time... Sebastian is on a short lease. He's been trying to bully his way around lately, a lot of our friends are tired of it.

Bonita: okay.

Diego: when will I see u again me love?

Bonita: soon...

She placed the phone down on the floor then placed both hands on the side of her head. Bonita didn't want to do it but she had too. Diego was her last resort if she or Naseem couldn't fix it. Diego had a lot of connections that included suppliers, death squads, military and foreign government officials and CIA helpers. He was well-connected with the underground figures that secretly controlled epic enterprises that ran the globe.

Diego also was infatuated with Bonita. And, she had feelings for him but she never took it any further than a few dinners and a lot of flirting. She loved Naseem. But, she had to flirt with Diego in order to have a little advantage over the competition.

Luis had taught her a long time ago that a pretty face, a mesmerizing frame and intelligence could take her a long way in life. Not just in the drug business but also in the corporate world too. It wasn't nothing more alluring to a powerful man than a woman who had beauty and brains.

Bonita listened, intently, to the pointers that her father also tried to give her in life and they worked just like he said they would. Bonita took a deep breath before raising her head and displaying a huge smile on her face.

Chapter 12

The soft white landed then soared through the City of Chester and surrounding areas. The appearance of it was bringing back some lost and forgotten years of glory for Chester.

The City had been known since the early 60's to produce some of the slickest and richest hustlers in the tri-state. With the names of such as Brother Price, Asmar, Slick Rick, Shamms', Harp and Dareen Majeed. These were some of the forefathers who set the mode and pace to get down and dirty for the money in the streets. And, the young hustlers of the latter years tried to follow their path. Some did it, and many, many others had failed.

But that all was going to come to an end. Especially, if the Brothers had a say so in the matter.

With Destiny remaining true to her word she dropped a heavy load on the Brothers. And, the Brothers being true hustlers knew exactly what to do with it. They made it work and ran through it fast.

"How you feeling this new flow?" Tate asked Idris.

The two were bending the corner of 2nd and Thurlow. They had been riding around all morning looking at property. Tate was trying to invest in real estate. And, what area was better than around Harrah's casino, so he figured.

Abandon homes and buildings ran up and down 2nd street. Which was heavy with traffic but nobody seemed to want to invest in the dilapidated area. They didn't want the headache of turning nothing into something except Tate. He had seen the vision and opportunity when nobody else did. Shortly before the Harrah's casino was built a lot of the white slum lords were canvassing the area trying to buy up the blacks homes. They wouldn't sell. The first reason being that they didn't trust them. And, the second reason was that most of the slum lords were trying to pull out all types of illegal schemes and scams to get the properties little to nothing. But times got hard and changed for the worst. This was true even for most residents of Chester. The murder rate was shooting up, more drugs were floating around and people were taking flight from the area. And, Tate was going to be there to capitalize off of this sudden change of heart.

His goal was to purchase the homes then sell them in a nice package deal or, if that didn't work out he thought about knocking the homes down then leasing the land to the City or Harrah casino to do whatever they wanted with it. He didn't care but either way Tate would benefit and make a nice profit or steady cash flow.

"Old head, money starting to jump. I've never seen it coming like this in a while."

"I know... I remember back when we were youngbuls that this was how it use to come... But, that's when everybody had money. It wasn't nothing to see the old heads riding around in the 850's, 640's, Porsches, 190 Benz's... Man since I came home, I only seen a few niggas getting paper and got a foreign." Tate said then started shaking his head. It was sad. The youth had totally changed. It wasn't about getting rich no more. Everybody was trying to kill and kill for the stupidest reasons.

They continued riding around viewing homes then Tate headed to the highway. He had to go to McDonalds and meet a friend.

On the way Tate schooled Idris through the whole ride. He was trying to mold the young hitter. He had seen a lot potential in Idris but nobody had ever tried to bring it out of him. But, Tate would.

Tate got off the exit at Chi-Chester and drove through the green light into the McDonalds parking lot. It was right around noon time so the fast-food restaurant was being rushed with a barrage of hungry customers. This was great for Tate and the business he planned on attending too.

He found a parking space and threw the SUV in park.

"Yo man, this nigga straight you got me meeting?"

"Old head, the bul good... I be fucking his little sister and he cut into me like that. But, bul be hitting the road to sell his work." Right after Idris made this statement a tan Cherokee pulled on the side of Tate's white Denali.

"This, the nigga?" Tate asked and gave a little head nod to the left of him.

Idris leaned up from the passenger side, a little bit to peer down in the car. "Yeah, that's the nigga Tray driving but I don't know that nigga on the passenger side... He looked familiar but I don't know ol' head."

Tate stared at the passenger to but couldn't recognize him. Tray got out of the car then stepped over to the driver's door. Tate rolled the window down when he approached.

Tray raised his hand then stuck it in the window of the Yukon. "Yo, what's up Tate? It's good that I finally get to meet you... You know that your rep precedes you, so I just want to say that I respect the path y'all laid for us... Putting the city on the map and all of that type of shit."

Tate smiled then replied, "don't believe everything you hear, my nigga."

"It's all good... Anyway though, I hear that y'all got it and I'm trying to grab like ten real quick... But, if the price is right and its good I'm going to need like twenty by the end of the week."

"Yo, dig this my nigga I don't fuck wit that shit but I got a few youngbuls that I could put you on... I don't know they might be able to fill that order... You know the bul just coming home. I'm just fucking with real estate right now." Tate said with a smile.

He had caught a gut feeling from Tray's comments and approach. Tate

111

didn't want to deal with him and he was trying to tell Tray that in a diplomatic way.

"Ae, where you be at anyway? I haven't seen you around the city before."

"I be here and there... But I got people that I serve in Wilmington, Pittsburg, NC and Maryland... I get around."

"Yo, the bul from the city too?" Tate asked pointing to the passenger.

Tray turned around and glanced at Shitty. "Oh, that's my man Shitty. He from over the eastside by Sleepy Hollows."

Tate remained quiet. The statement had sealed the deal with Tray. Tate wouldn't be serving him nor would any of his young buls. Shitty was a bitch. A snake. A rat. A confidential informant for the federal government, and a stone-cold killer. A deadly mix.

"My nigga, I'm good... I heard about the bul... Forget about the part when I said my young bul might got it."

"Damn nigga its like that! Yo, that's the word around the city about you niggas. You niggas act like y'all don't want to serve nobody an all that shit... What the fuck you niggas on!" Tray replied with an attitude that caught Shitty's attention.

Idris reached under his shirt then slide his hand on the black Sig Sauer. But before he could fully brandish it Tate spoke. "Nigga, we ain't fucking wit no rat ass niggas... Back the fuck up nigga." Tate said with a menacing face. All of the pent up frustration of life and from being in prison for so many years came out of him. And, Tray definitely could pick up on the jail tone that Tate voiced.

Unable to take the disrespect, Tate smacked the shit out of Tray. He stumbled back to his car.

Idris raised the .40 up then tried to stretch across Tate. "Put that shit the fuck up nigga." He yelled at Idris then yanked off out of the parking spot.

Tray had regained his balance and ran around the car to the driver side. But, Shitty leaped out of the car then raised a Ruger and let off two shots towards the Yukon pulling out of the parking lot.

"Hurry up! Hurry up! Get in the fucking truck." Tray yelled at Shitty.

Tray was steaming. Tate had totally disrespected him. But, Tray wasn't going for it. He didn't care who he was or the reputation that he carried for murdering people in broad daylight over some petty beef. He wanted revenge and he wanted it now. Tray wasn't going to wait until he seen Tate again or wait around in order to lay on Tate—no.

He sped out of the McDonalds parking lot. By that time, Tate had made a left and was on the highway going in the direction of I-95 North.

Tray punched it trying to catch up to the Denali.

Shitty sat on the passenger side waiting for the perfect opportunity to dump on the SUV in traffic. But, the small Cherokee SUV was no match for the big Yukon. Shitty seen that then picked up his phone. He yelled, "NC", in the phone. It dialed a number and the person picked up on the first ring.

"Where you at?" Shitty asked, in a concern tone.

"On the highway coming from Philly."

"What part? I need you real quick."

"I'm just passing the airport."

"Bet! Look, we just got into it wit that nutt-ass nigga Tate from the Gardens . He just smacked the bul... We trying to see this nigga now."

"Where you at?"

Tate reached the Highland Avenue exit ramp. He slowed down a bit to round the turn then punched it when he seen no cars at the bottom of the hill and the light green.

"Nigga, don't every do no shit like that... I got this... No fucking killing in public while I'm fucking driving! Don't ever do that shit!" Tate snapped out and told Idris.

He wasn't trying to go back to prison. Especially for a stupid ass murder. Tate knew it was a better way to skin a nigga. And, killing one in public wasn't it. It might set the tone and send a message to others that them gangstas from Killa Hill still wasn't going for nothing and that they would still kill at will but that would start a whole new investigation like back in his Boyle Street days.

"These niggas following us... I'm going up the way. Call Hak and Meer then tell them to get ready."

Idris hurried up and made the call. Hak answered on the first ring.

"These niggas think we sweet... Hak and Meer up there and ready to move?"

"Yeah!" Idris said, while looking back at the car chasing them.

Tate took off down Townshipline Road then went through the light and down the one-way street on Renshaw Road.

Shitty remained quiet and studied the situation. He had been in plenty of gun fights and this one was no different.

Tate shook his head then said, "I can't believe I got this rat ass nigga chasing me... Sheesh!"

He didn't mention it yet but Tate was also heated at Idris for even placing him in this predicament. Idris was raised and groomed up in the Highland Gardens so therefore he should've known the history of Shitty. And, if he didn't know the history, he should've known that he was the undisputed leader of the B.A.M. squad. Everybody in Chester knew this.

The story of the sucker Shitty was legendary in Chester and how he murdered an official hustler who had been once crowned king in the city.

Shitty had been a youngster that was raised on the streets and by a straight goon who played by all the rules. But, all of that molding and stand-up character that he displayed would be wiped away due to his vicious betrayal of the life he chose. This happened right after catching a Fed case.

The indictment arose out of a conspiracy that stretched from Chester to Miami, Florida. Shitty had played a minor role in the conspiracy but still faced a mandatory minimum sentence of 20 years. This was due to the fact he had one prior drug conviction as a youth..After realizing that he could spend 20 years behind a concrete wall for his minor role, Shitty broke and cooperated with the government which helped bring down the head of the conspiracy.

In the fourth year of incarceration, Shitty got word that his father, Stone, had been murdered by an up-and-coming gangster—lil Nigga.

After mourning the death and realizing why he got killed, Shitty had respected the fact that lil Nigga had murdered Stone. But, lil Nigga had went too far, he thought, by setting him on fire.

Stone had killed lil Nigga's father back in the day when he was still a kid. Lil Nigga had sought revenge and achieved it.

Even though, Shitty had cooperated with the government and became a stool pigeon, Stone still took care of his son. He kept money on Shitty's books and visited when he could. So, he plotted day and night on evening the score with lil Nigga.

After finishing up his five year sentence, Shitty headed to Charlotte, North Carolina to link up with his new partner Troy who also was a snitch.

On their first move together Troy went to settle a score with his baby mother for betraying him. She had violated the rule of going against him for some outsiders and helped some of the Jamaicans discredit him at trial. This incident almost caused Troy to lose his plea agreement.

By helping the Jamaicans out, they put Troy's baby mother in control of moving large amounts of marijuana. They had continued to flood the city, even while they were in jail.

Troy set her up. He got Shitty to pose as an out-of-town buyer of some weight. Shitty had kidnapped her and the two took all of her weed and slaughtered her. They headed to Chester after the murder to unload the weed and settle the score with lil Nigga.

He laid low and planned daily on the boys called the Young Gunz. Shitty caught lil Nigga's stepfather coming out of his store and ambushed him with his squad. The crew hit Saleem over thirteen times with AR's. Troy had tried to finish off the rest of Saleem's sons and nephew, but was caught off guard by Saleem's niece. Amina ran out of the store with a shotgun and hit Troy square in the neck. He died instantly at the scene. Shitty and the squad left him to die alone on the gritty street.

Troy brother, Mike took the death hard. Although he was young at the time, Mike vowed to avenge his brother's death. He was mad at the world and hated everything that came out of the City of Chester except of course his man, Shitty.

After going back and forth with killing each other men, Shitty decided to leave Chester for a little bit. He went back down to Charlotte, and hooked up with Mike. They had been hanging tuff ever since. Around this same time Shitty cousin came down.

Stan had come up with a nice lick for the crew. It was a simple and easy one that could be done in the City of Charlotte.

Major leased a condominium for his baby sister, Reeka and her friend

-Tish to live in. They had a job working on a cruise ship that imported drugs for Polo and Priest. So, Major had used the place as a stash house and a place to rest when he was down in NC to oversee the unloading of the drugs coming off the ship.

Shitty and Mike plotted on the two divas for months.

They had finally got a break one night, and the girls asked them to come back to the condo. When Shitty and Mike got there they tried to rob them but the plot got foiled. Tish got shot several times and lived. Reeka didn't get shot. She got out of the condo then ran outside to the parking lot looking for help from anybody. Stan acted fast and hit her with the car. The three home invaders dashed away in to the dark night and left the two women to die.

The trio got away and ran back up north to Philly where they scored another big lick. They had robbed and killed Major's partner Chance.

After months of investigating the incident, Major got a big break and found out who lined his sister up. Major caught one of them. He blew Stan brains out, and has been searching for Shitty and Mike ever since.

"Ol' head, they set up..."

"Aight! Aight!" Tate replied as he was pulling on to Highland Avenue coming off of 12th Street.

Tray was right behind him but Shitty wouldn't shoot this time. Shitty was waiting for the perfect chance to hit Tate. Just their luck, no vehicles were passing or going on the two lane street. A few motorists were at the light but they had seen the high accelerated vehicles coming and didn't move.

"Yo, where you at?" Shitty yelled in the phone to Mike who had stayed on the line.

"I'm coming over the bridge now, the one off of Highland Avenue exit." Mike said.

"We chasing him ya way... You should see the white Yukon any minute and we right behind."

Tate was flying down the empty street. He approached the light at the top of Township Line Road. A few cars were at this intersection also but none moved when they seen the speeding vehicles. Mike had just made it to the corner. He rolled the window down then slung out a huge Desert Eagle .50 caliber pistol out of the window. "Boom! Boom! Boom!"

Tate seen the weapon come out of the window. He swerved a little bit but didn't break his stride.

Mike banged the U-turn then followed Tray.

Tate faked as if he was getting back on the highway but banged a hard right which led into Killa Hill. Tray and Mike fail for the bait. They followed Tate in to the hood.

"Watch this?" Tate said, while staring out of the rear view. He wanted to see if they still were going to follow him in the middle of the development.

Tate stormed up Culhane Street but right before Tray could past Kane Street, Womp jumped in the street and threw a brick at Tray's window. He didn't see it coming because he was so bent on catching Tate.

The brick smashed through the driver side window. Tray slammed on the breaks. Mike rammed in the back of him and caused Tray to run in to a parked car. All hell broke loose after that.

Hak and Meer ran off of the 2600 block of Nolan Street with assault rifles in their hands. They had all black on and wore clown masks.

The two spared the vehicles no mercy. Hak ran down on Tray's SUV while Meer dashed up on Mike's. "Blap! Blap! Blap! Blap! Blap!" The gun fire could be heard for blocks around the huge gritty area.

The young hitters sprayed the vehicles. Hak dropped over 50 rounds into the SUV. It wasn't a place on the vehicles that didn't get hit. And, Meer did the same with Mike's truck.

Hak and Meer had shredded the vehicles to pieces then dashed off back down the street. They jogged through the alleyway then on to Ward Street where they hopped in a getaway truck.

Tate spun the corner. He drove up but stopped in the middle of Culhane Street. He couldn't believe it. It was packed.

The whole neighborhood had heard the shots and came out to see damage.

The group was done. Hak and Meer had handled the business and finished the job. Mike, Shitty and Tray were laid out in their vehicles with blood and bullet holes everywhere.

This would be the first triple murder in the neighborhood in a few years. With over 90 rounds of shells all over the pavement and kilos of cocaine flowing through the hood Killa Hill was back to its old tricks. Killa Hill was back to living up to its name, and fulfilling its destiny, as the land of the lost souls.

Destiny

Chapter 13

"Y'all know the difference right between rap facts and fiction right!" Jay Z's song. I got the keys blasted through the club, as the whole crowd sang word-for-word with the song.

A large flat screen was suspended from the air and hung in the middle of the dance floor. The bar stood to the side with liquor filling the racks, and an Ace design stood in the background made by gold and black bottles of liquor. This was an exquisite design but nobody paid attention to it. Especially on this particular night because most of the people in the club was intoxicated by either liquor or drugs.

The crowd was thick and the Big Apple's finest along with a mixture of other celebrities like entertainers, athletes, and major underground figures were in attendance. The big event had been thrown together at the last minute, and was for the Brooklyn Nets successful playoff victory against the Knicks. After the game everybody was directed, via social media and word-of-mouth, to head to the after-party being thrown by New York's ambassador Jay Z. He held it in Manhattan at his exclusive club called 40/40.

Jigga had the drinks flowing with an open bar, and this included the VIP sections of the club where Major's entourage were parked at.

He stood up, at the front of the VIP section overlooking the main floor, with a black bottle of D'usse. Major was tossing it back as if it was water. He didn't care that these bottles weren't included in the open bar theme of the club. Major still had to pay for everyone that he brought to the club and that reached to the teens.

Major accepted this because tonight they were celebrating. Not for the Nets as the others were celebrating for but for Shitty and Mike's demise.

He had been on Shitty and Mike line for years. But, they had proved to be elusive, and the other thing that contributed to his failure to catch up with them was because of his fugitive status. The Feds were still searching for him.

Major had been skipping towns and going from city-to-city dodging the alphabet boys. He would stay in Atlanta for a year or two then move on to LA for the same amount of time, and the list goes on. All the while, he was still getting to the money.

Establishing connections, politicking with other bosses about the drug trade, and setting up businesses in case that destined date would come and he'd be shipped to federal prison.

He wasn't scared about going to prison nor did he fear the time that the Feds were trying to give him, Major just wanted to kill the one witness who could tie him to the case.

Polo was finishing out his sentence, and he was the only person who could tie Major to anything. Murders, home invasions, and the distribution of multiple kilos that occurred over a five year period. Major needed Polo dead. But, he couldn't kill him until Polo touched the streets. So, he had to dodge the feds until then.

Major nodded his head to the lyrics of the music. He was in a nostalgic mood tonight. "I got the keys, the keys, I got the keys... Major key alert!" He yelled to the crowd but they couldn't hear him. Major was turned up at the late hour.

He turned around to the others gathered around the mid-size VIP section. A black leather sectional ran across the back of the room while a mini-bar stood to the side, and a flat screen hung on the other side.

Major turned all the way around. He was dressed in an all black Armani t-shirt and jeans with a nice size diamond necklace. Major topped it off with a pair of black Prada sneakers.

He pointed at Tate who was seated in the back, on the sectional with Meeka sitting on his lap and her feet dangling between his legs. The lovely brown skin diva had on a red mini-skirt with black heels. She was stunning and setting it out for the big fella. This was her way of saying thank you, so she thought.

Major just stared at the couple. He didn't care that his baby sister was all over Tate. He had put her on Tate.

Tate caught Major pointing at him so he raised his bottle of D'usse up, in order to salute the D-boy.

Jay seen him pointing, and raised his bottle too, but went back to hollering at Destiny. She was seated next to him in a tight white mini-skirt. Destiny looked sexy and edible. And, Jay wanted to see just how nice that body appeared with the skirt off.

Destiny had been flirting from time-to-time with the goon but tried to compose herself around the crew and play it lady like. For the simple reason that, she didn't want the small entourage to think that Jay had a shot at getting cozy with the boss later on tonight.

Destiny was feeling lonely and upset. She had been fuming over the issue with Naseem and couldn't shake the fact that she had to make a tuff decision. Destiny didn't want to be involved with no police or government agency. But, Naseem was dragging her into the web. First, by being the group leader who had the last approval on who supplied them. And, second, she was falling in love with him. Destiny wanted to get away from both of those scenarios, and Jay was her first chance to probably help her relieve all the pain and stress from this predicament.

Jay was Destiny's first choice to help her once again save the day. And, if he didn't know it yet, Destiny was intrigued by his gangsta. He was different she thought. Jay was reserved but commanded respect by his silence and demanded to be rich.

Destiny held the glass up filled with pink Rozay. She drank a little sip while staring at Jay with the glassy eyes. She leaned over, so nobody else could hear and whispered in his ear. "You're coming with me tonight!"

It wasn't a question for Jay to answer but more like an order or demand. Jay smiled then glanced over at Major who was eyeing the two.

Jay didn't respond to her question slash order. He just laid back and took the whole scene in. Jay was enjoying the moment. He had came a long way from sitting in a 6x9 cell reading and dreaming about being rich and having the freedom to do as he pleased. He did 15 years of it. Now, Jay's visions and dreams became a reality. He had a plug, plenty of money, freedom, and a vicious squad of young hitters to provide a smooth path to the road to riches.

Idris stood up with a black bottle in his left hand and Dutch in the other. He was high out of his mind but the loving the scene. This was new territory for the hitter but he planned to take full advantage of the opportunity. He stepped over and sat next to the gorgeous Tish.

Tish had been dancing and drinking heavy. She was overwhelmed by the death of Shitty and Mike. They had finally got what they deserved.

The high yellow diva wore a forest green leather long sleeve skirt by Oscar de la Renta. She was trying to catch a Big Willie tonight. If, it wasn't for Destiny, the ex-model, lounging in the VIP section, Tish would've surely took the show over tonight. But, Destiny had her beat. That didn't stop the young hitters from Killa Hill trying to lean on Tish though. At first, she wasn't going for it. But, Jay wasn't paying her any attention and that's who she really was shooting for. So, the young hitter kept going at her. Idris had finally worn her down and she was all game now.

Tish didn't usually go for the young boys but Idris had something else going on for him. He was accepted and respected amongst the Kings from what she had seen throughout the night. Idris was frontin' though. He was playing the game on a mental level tonight. Idris knew that thug shit wouldn't work around certain sophisticated older women; especially the broads that had been around niggas with real money and real goals. Tish was one of those women.

Idris appeared like money tonight. He had a black t-shirt on that had Garden Boy Savage across the front in white, Louis Vuitton denim jeans and some black Louis Vuitton sneakers. She knew he was frontin' for the night but rolled with the act because she knew eventually that the young boy would have his turn one day to rule. And, she didn't want him to forget about her when he did.

Idris sat down next to Tish. She was in a bubbly mood, and planned on giving the young hitter a night to remember.

Major still feeling the cognac effects motioned for everybody to gather around. At the time, Meer, Hak, Tyson, Womp and Muscle were coming through the VIP section. They had a couple of their young buls with them. The group headed straight to the back with Idris, Jay and Tate.

Destiny, and everybody else got up. They stood in the middle of the room. Major raised the black bottle with XO on it in white and mentioned, "to success... I wish this team much success... We going to do it epic this year... You best believe that... So let's toast to success."

The whole VIP section raised their black bottles and glasses then toasted. This was the beginning. Major had full trust in the Chester boys who had proved to be loyal, brave and reliable. And, for this trust and also for murdering Shitty and Mike, Major gave the young hitters two kilos a piece. It was a small gesture of his gratitude for them and to show that he respected their loyalty by taking care of his problem.

The young hitters loved the reward and accepted it even after the brothers told them that they shouldn't accept the gift. They told them not to accept the bricks because Shitty and Mike got hit it for their disrespectful act of shooting at Tate. And, in addition to that, the brothers said that accepting money for murdering was for suckas not for real niggas. Real niggas handled their own beefs. The young buls understood their concerns but they reminded the brothers that at the end of the day, they were riding for them and that's all they cared about. They didn't care about Major and didn't owe him any type of loyalty so why not take the free shit that he was dishing out.

Destiny signaled for Major to step to the side. He came over then leaned close to her. She whispered and stated that, "get the brothers, so we could talk upstairs in the private room."

Major stepped off and got the brothers together while Destiny strutted out of the VIP section with Brucie in the flank.

Brucie stood outside of the door as Major, Tate and Jay stepped up to the VIP section on the second floor.

This was a secluded area that had been reserved for private parties, if you didn't want to be bothered with the crowd downstairs. It was super exclusive and only a few people had them tonight. Mostly were entertainers who didn't want to party with locals. And, the other occupants were trap stars. The trap stars who were having their own private extravaganzas in the rooms.

Destiny stood in the middle of the floor trying to gain her composure. She was tipsy but still on point.

The brothers stepped in followed by Major. Destiny turned around and waved them over to her. They got closer, then Destiny spoke first. "I would like to say that everything is going smooth and according to plan... But, we might have a problem."

"What?" Major asked.

Destiny just stared at him. She was about to reveal the problem but decided against it. The time wasn't right, she thought. Destiny decided at that moment that she needed to think a little bit more about it. "Polo will be coming home soon, and I don't want to have anything to do with him... He may try to sabotage everything because of that."

"Don't worry I'm going to take care of Polo... I've been waiting to get even with him for years." Major said then turned to the brothers. "I just want to say thank you again for that favor y'all did for me."

"What's done is done... We don't have to keep dwelling on that or talkin bout that either." Tate replied. He hated the fact that after Shitty and Mike were killed, Major kept thanking them and talking about the murders. That type of stuff spooked the brothers. They didn't play that shit. Real niggas didn't talk about past or present murders in casual settings. So, by the fact that Major kept bringing it up had them kinda looking at him sideways. They knew about the work he had put in and all the other gangsta shit that he was involved in. But, Major still had an open indictment. They had experienced firsthand on how the federal government could break some of the stone cold criminals. And, Major wasn't exempt from it. He hadn't been battled tested yet, so on that level he was still suspect.

"Nah, playa it ain't nothing like that... Yo, I'm one hunna, bru... So, we going to leave it like that." Major felt the vibes that the brothers were throwing at him. And, he knew that if he didn't check it now, and set the record straight that there would always be a cloud of suspicion over the top of his head. He wasn't going to let that happen. Major had killed too many rats, suckas, robbers and other niggas for him to be looked at like that.

"Look I have a very important thing going on with this group. We're meeting this week and if it doesn't look right... I might need y'all to clean up a few things for me."

They knew what she meant by 'clean up' a few things. Major was all for it but not the brothers. They weren't guns for hire. The brothers were trying to leave that aspect of the game alone. You couldn't kill and get wealthy. They learnt that lesson the hard way. But, if imprisonment was involved in Destiny's concerns or problems then cleaning up had to be done.

"What's wrong Destiny? Are they pushing you to do something or is there an informant in the circle?" Major asked with a curious face.

"No, but I'll keep y'all informed... I just wanted to say thank you... To all three of y'all for helping me get rid of this material rather quickly." She said then gave Major a hug. Destiny followed up with Tate next but stopped when she got to Jay.

"Excuse me, could I have a moment with Jay only? I'll catch up with y'all downstairs in a second."

Major nodded his head then headed for the exit. Major didn't like the ideal of Destiny getting cozy with Jay and she seen that when he turned around before stepping out of the door.

She promised herself to talk to Major about that.

Tate followed Major out of the door then went downstairs.

The door closed behind Tate. Destiny stepped closer to Jay. The liquor had her fearless, willing and vulnerable. She had been holding back the urge all night to be embraced by the gangsta. And, the only thing that stopped her was the perception that she thought the crew would have towards her sexing a member of the group. Destiny didn't want them to think she was a thot or anything like that. So, she had to be discreet with her actions and feelings.

Jay towered over the petite woman. She wasn't intimated by this. Destiny leaned a little closer and stood on her tippy-toes to give Jay a kiss, as she embraced him.

Jay bent down and kissed the exotic woman on the lips while he felt all over her body. Destiny loved it. She wanted it and wanted it now.

Destiny pushed Jay backed then got up on the table. She waved him over as she pulled up her skirt. She didn't have any panties on, and her nice size vagina, which was cleanly shaved, poked out like a little muffin.

Jay got closer to Destiny but didn't make a move. He wanted Destiny to make the first move. Jay wanted her to take control. He knew she wanted it so he decided to play his cards right.

Destiny grabbed Jay by his YSL belt buckle then started unbuckling his denim jeans. She got them loose and tried to push them down along with his boxer briefs. She couldn't.

Jay pulled down his briefs then stepped closer to Destiny. She grabbed his hard love maker then stroked on it a few times.

Destiny slide the nine inches up in her; she closed her eyes and moaned lightly. She loved it, and didn't feel any remorse for what she just done.

She was secure within herself. Destiny knew that just because she gave up the goodies to Jay so quickly that it didn't make her a whore. Destiny just wanted what she wanted, and she always got what she wanted no matter what. And, Destiny wanted Jay as a friend, lover and business partner. So, Destiny set out to achieve all of the above because Naseem was history. At least, he was history to her. Naseem would never get another shot to lay with the coffee color diva.

Chapter 14

The morning sun shined through the window. Destiny entered the room and went straight to the fridge in order to grab a drink. She grabbed a bottle of a water then headed back to the living room and sat down on the sofa. Destiny snatched her phone off the small glass table. She scanned through her emails then on to her social media accounts. "Oh, my God!" Was all that she said. She didn't want to believe it.

Destiny had just found out, via text, that all of her private information like being the owner, president and CEO of the Jones Foundation, and other companies that she had acquired since joining forces with the group had been leaked to the public. Social media had been buzzing about Destiny's little secret.

Admires, friends, and strangers were leaving tweets and posts about the fact that they couldn't understand how a model could have accumulated so much wealth in such a short period, and didn't commit a crime by doing so. Some even dried snitched and accused her of selling some type of illegal drugs.

Destiny couldn't believe what she was seeing. Naseem had set her up with some professionals who were experts at hiding money, assets and companies from the public. He hooked Destiny up with Omar Mossack who created a shell company for her. Destiny had placed her company and the company that was structured under a Trust that was left to her to control by Polo and Priest, in a secret shell company that was named after her favorite aunt. So, Destiny didn't understand how the stuff got leaked. But, she needed to find out.

She tried to set up a meeting with Naseem, in order to get to the bottom of the issue because it needed to be fixed, immediately. But, Naseem couldn't make it and this infuriated Destiny even more. She had a major crisis on her hands that could potentially harm the other members of the group, and Naseem didn't have time to take her meeting. So, Destiny placed a call with Omar Mossack, and he agreed to meet, as soon as possible. Destiny then arranged to fly over to Panama in order to discuss the problem. But despite Omar's agreement to meet, Destiny felt something was wrong and she needed to get to the bottom of it. Destiny did some searching by calling around to the other members and came up with some vital information on Naseem and Omar.

Destiny found that Naseem had a daughter by Bonita Matta. The daughter of the infamous Luis Matta who distributed a huge percentage of drugs in the United States and aboard.

The revelation that Naseem had child with Bonita wasn't surprising. It all made sense to Destiny now. Naseem had slithered his way into the Matta family, and was trying to help them corner the cocaine market in the United States.

Destiny laid across the sofa with an iPhone in her hands. She was scrolling through her Instagram account when a text came through by Bonita.

Bonita: I'm walking through your hallway. Can you please open your door?

Destiny: Open my door, who are you?

She replied trying to play it off. Destiny couldn't believe that Bonita knew where she lived, and was coming to her private sanctuary.

Destiny leaped up off the couch. She ran to the long mirror and checked her appearance. Everything was intact. Destiny had just finished working out. Her hair was in a bun, and she still had on her workout gear. A pink sports bra and black spandex pants with pink, black and white Nike's on her feet.

Bonita: I'm Naseem's finance... And, we have a mutual problem that needs to be discussed so open the door I'm standing out front.

Destiny headed over to the door and glanced out of the peephole. Bonita stood there with two bulky bodyguards standing in back of her.

Destiny hesitated for a second. She didn't know what to expect.

Destiny didn't know if Bonita was coming to have her murdered for having an affair with Naseem. She had heard about how ruthless the Matta family could get when family was involved. But, Destiny couldn't understand that, if Bonita was coming to murder her why would she come through the main hallway and risk being seen on the Condo's surveillance system.

She decided to let Bonita in. Destiny wanted to know, exactly, what business was it that they had a mutual problem that needed to be fixed. It couldn't have been about Naseem, and if it was than Bonita was in for a rude awakening. Destiny had been made up her mind that Naseem was finished. History. Destiny didn't want any type of relationship with a potential collaborator with the government.

Destiny swung the door open. Bonita stood there and sized Destiny up and down. She was trying to figure out what Naseem had seen in her. And, when Bonita made her, personal, inventory of Destiny she seen exactly what Naseem seen. Destiny was a model. Her youthful and exquisite appearance spoke volumes. This along with those Arabian and Jamaican features.

Bonita turned to her two Hispanic bodyguards, and said something in Spanish. She then asked Destiny, "may I come in?"

"Sure... But, only you... I don't know you or those two men with you."

"It's okay, I already told them that I was going by myself. Even though, they disagree." She replied with a fake smile.

Bonita stepped in the foray of the place. She glanced around trying to observe the home.

Destiny closed the door then locked it. She turned then gave Bonita a quick look over. Everything about Bonita exuded power and elegance. She was a woman with an upper-class demeanor and education but had a ruffless edge. Bonita had dressed down today but still appeared extremely appealing. She had on a pair of cotton cropped jeans and a multi-colored sweater with the sleeves rolled up to her elbows and tan

Gucci boots.

Bonita had turned and caught Destiny observing her. The two locked eyes and tried to hide the jealous and envy in their heart. Naseem had both of these extremely powerful women, in their own right, in his triangle of love. And, the key to conquering this was the fact that Naseem had managed to dig deep in to their hearts and minds. Destiny broke the silence and spoke.

"So, what can I do for you?"

"Maybe, we should have a seat... This might take a little time to figure out and understand."

Destiny stepped off and waved Bonita over to the sofa. They both took a seat.

"I'm pretty sure you know my fiancé, Naseem..."

"Yes." Destiny replied by trying to say little, as possible. Destiny wanted her to do all the talking and explaining.

"Well, before I began, I want to show you something."

Bonita reached in her Burkin bag then pulled out her phone. She strolled through a few things then handed Destiny the phone.

Destiny's nude picture in Hong Kong was the first picture that appeared on the screen. She didn't feel embarrassed by it. Destiny was a model so being undressed in front of men and women who sometimes she didn't know or just met didn't bother her. What did bother her was the fact that Bonita had it.

Destiny didn't flinch when she seen it. She continued to scroll through the photos. Destiny came across a quite few of them. She didn't say a thing after seeing them. Destiny handed Bonita the phone back. Bonita accepted the phone from her then stated, "I'm not here because of this affair that you're having with Naseem. I could care less at this point... This is bigger than you fucking my fiancé... By the way, did you know this?"

"I asked him was he involved with anyone and he told me no... I don't share men nor do I have sex with them if they're in a relationship."

Bonita didn't bother to dwell on the last comment. But it did just confirm her suspicions. "A person by the name of Sebastian emailed me those pictures... Do you know him or did you ever meet him?"

"I don't know him, and I don't think I've ever seen this man... Do you have a picture of him?"

Bonita searched through her phone than found it. She turned the phone around so Destiny could see the photo.

"Yes, I've seen him when we were in Hong Kong... I was standing in the hotel's hallway when Naseem was talking to him in the living room."

"In Hong Kong? Did you hear what the conversation was about?"

"I'm sorry but I don't want to be rude. But, why are you asking me about this? This has nothing to do with me having an affair with Naseem."

"Well, your right about the affair part but this person is the one who leaked your info to the public... Have you heard of the Panama papers?"

"Yes..."

The Panama Papers is what the news reporters had dubbed the biggest leak. This leak had an enormous effect on business and world leaders. It had been widely speculated by the public that it had been the actions of the CIA but this accusation still hadn't been proven.

"Okay, this man, Sebastian, is the one responsible for this leak... A leak that has affected me, you, and a lot of our other partners." Bonita stated, hoping that Destiny got the bigger picture. "Do you understand, now?"

Destiny shook her head while answering, "Yes, I completely understand now... All of the pieces seem to be coming together."

"I understand that Naseem introduced you to Omar Mossack who created a few shell companies for you... Well, that's how I found out about you... Omar informed me that an American woman was coming to Panama to see him so I did some digging on you. . . I had thought you were with CIA then I received these photos from Sebastian, and my suspicions went up."

"Your suspicions went up for what? I don't know this man."

"I understand you don't know him but he's a dangerous man... He works for the CIA. Did you know this?"

"No..." Destiny stated with conviction. She remained strong but her whole world just collapsed around her.

Destiny didn't imagine that she was this deep into the business. She wanted out. "Well, how do I distance myself from this?" Destiny wanted out and she planned on getting out, quickly.

"It's not that easy. But, I can help... That's why I asked you what did this man say to Naseem."

"Look..." Bonita stopped her before Destiny could finish the thought.

"I know you've heard about my family being murdered?"

"I seen it on the news... I didn't personally connect the two with Naseem and you but I've seen it."

"Well, I control all of the family's business... And, this includes the one your associated with."

"Okay." Destiny said, and understood than that Bonita was running the show on an epic level.

"So please tell me what this man said."

"He was talkin' about helping Naseem take control over the US market, if Naseem helped him get control of some port area."

Bonita was stunned by the answer. Naseem had never spoke about this meeting with her. This was unusual for Naseem. The two had been working as a team for well over six years, and they never kept secrets from each other.

"Are you sure this is what the conversation was about?"

"Yes, Sebastian also said that if he didn't comply that he would cause a lot of pain and suffering to Naseem's family."

Bonita sat back then crossed her legs. Sebastian was trying to set a trap and play the two against each other.

"How do you feel about this?" Bonita asked. She wanted to get a sense of direction or an understanding of where Destiny stood at with all of this mess.

"Excuse me, I still didn't get your name?"

"Bonita... Bonita Matta." She replied then stuck out her manicured hand out for Destiny.

They shook hands then Destiny went on to say that, "as I sit here and hear you ask these questions, I was thinking the same about you. Where do you stand? Well, I'm pretty sure you know about the group and all that we're trying to accomplish... Anyway, I stated to them before I accepted to be in this elite group that I did not want to be involved with law enforcement... Naseem knew this, and he promised me that we wouldn't be dealing with any government agents... So when I stumbled upon the conversation in Hong Kong I was taken aback... Truthfully, I've been planning to exit the business... I don't want to get caught up with them corrupt people. I've had a terrible experience with the government... My ex-boyfriend cooperated and snitched on his brother."

Bonita soaked the whole scene in. She knew vaguely about the incident but she loved Destiny's answer.

"I'm glad to hear that... Naseem has never told me about this visit. I think he was planning on working with them behind my back and yours. This is unacceptable!"

"Yes, it is."

"So there's still good news. I've got an excellent PR firm who can help with the shaky image that the Panama Papers tried to place on you. Would you like to use them?"

"Of course... My modeling career took me around the world where I've met a lot of important and influential people who I would love to do business with someday... I don't need this scandal tarnishing my reputation."

"Okay, I'll get them right on it... But, the question is what about Naseem. What do you have planned for him?"

"With all due respect to you... I'll let you handle it."

"Naseem is the father of my daughter so I don't want to exact any deadly punishment on him... I've decided to harm him financially, and strip him of position."

"What about if he decided to go with Sebastian?"

"I've got that problem with Sebastian getting taken care of soon so Naseem doesn't have any other powerful allies to work with beside the feds... And, I know for sure that he's not going to go with them."

Destiny frowned a bit. She didn't trust Naseem. He seemed weak to her. "But, I'm telling you, I don't trust Naseem. He lied to me throughout this whole ordeal."

Bonita understood her concerns. Naseem had crossed her when he cheated. Cheating was a cardinal sin to her, and this hurt Bonita the most. She understood why he didn't tell her about the meeting. Naseem wanted to control his own destiny. And, by removing Bonita he would fulfill that dream.

"I'll be staying in Panama for a while... And, I want you to take Naseem's spot inside the group... What do you think?'

"I'm not sure... I mean I got to speak with them first then see where everybody stands with this decision."

"I understand that but you need to be placed in that position... The Matta family has to be the sole supplier to the group... And, I know with you at the helm of this group that you could make that happen. Just visualize it... Two powerful women conquering a once male dominated positions in the business. This alone is historic, in and of itself."

Destiny didn't speak. She was trying to visualize the statement of Bonita. Destiny seen the bigger picture and loved it. But she didn't think that Naseem would resign so easily.

"I can understand and appreciate your vision for the future of this venture. But, I still have to run this past the group... Also, I don't think that Naseem will resign."

"Believe me, I've been dealing and sleeping with this man for a number of years. I know how to deal with him... I'll take care of it. Don't worry about it." Bonita said with a bit of sarcasm and jealousy.

Destiny caught the slight envy that Bonita displayed and, said when talking about Naseem. "Please, Bonita, you have to understand that I don't want your man... I've moved on."

Bonita smiled because she couldn't believe that Destiny caught the slight remarks. But, Bonita needed it to be understood that Destiny was to stay away from Naseem. He still was her daughter's father, and she had to have a relationship with him whether she forgave him or not.

"Destiny, I wasn't insinuating that you still wanted Naseem... I was just making a point to you." Bonita stated.

She was trying to cover up the obvious from Destiny. Bonita was still in love with Naseem.

"I wish you the best and I hope this smear campaign will be put to rest, soon... I'll call my PR team, as soon as I'm in the car." Bonita said then stood up from the sofa.

Destiny got up too then stepped around the table to meet Bonita. They shook hands then both headed to the door.

"I'm glad you stopped by and I'll talk to the others about the position..."

"Thank you... Please don't mention anything about the CIA. Naseem will inform them that he has resigned and he'll recommend you for the position."

"Why would he do that?"

"I'll make him an offer that he can't refuse." Bonita stated then gave a devilish grin to Destiny. She then opened the door and walked out.

Chapter 15

The blazing rays from the sun beamed down on the snow covered trees and grounds which gave off a scenic backdrop through the two enormous, floor-to-ceiling, windows. The long burgundy drapes had been pushed to the side, so it wouldn't obscure the view. The place hadn't been touched since Naseem held the first meeting in the room. Across from the window stood a huge oak cabinet with expensive china inside. A long table also decorated the center of the room with fifteen wooden chairs, with soft stuffed silk coverings, on each side and one at both ends.

Laptops sat neatly in front of each person seated around the table along with a folder, a glass cup, and a pitcher of water.

Destiny sat at the head of the table today. A large painting by Rembrandt hung on the wall behind Destiny. She also had a laptop, folders filled with documents and a water pitcher in front of her. Destiny studied the contents of the computer.

She was studying the speech that she had prepared for this particular occasion. Some of the other partners were concerned about the abrupt resignation of Naseem. They couldn't understand why he would just up and leave. Too much power, prestige and money was at stake for a person to just throw away.

Destiny peeked up from the laptop. Several of the partners were sitting there staring and trying to analyze the person, Destiny. Most of them were trying to grasp the reality that an ex-model had took the head of the group. Half of the members doubted her and were thinking about branching off and conducting business like the old days. Destiny needed to convince them otherwise.

She stood up from the chair. Destiny was always dressed immaculate. She had on a leather sleeveless dress. She was focused today. When,

Destiny last spoke with Bonita in Panama, she promised Bonita that business would go on as usual. Bonita was happy to hear that Destiny wanted to make it happen.

"Now, respected men and women, I know it's a lot of concern that you have with me being at the head of this table. But, as I spoke with most of you, individually, and I told y'all that I'm dedicated to this position and project..." She stated before stopping abruptly. Destiny was trying to get a feel of the audience while also showing strength and determination to win.

"So with that being the case, I've maintained the same ties with the Matta family... We have a direct link with the people that grow the raw material of cocaine... Therefore, our prices will be at a considerable low price."

"Yes, that's all fine and dandy. But what we're trying to figure out is why has Naseem resigned... We're hearing all of these rumors about this and that... I think as the heads or in the literal sense board members of this distribution network we have a right to know the truth." Crystal said with authority but delightful tone. She wanted to get down to business but she wanted to know the truth. Crystal admired Naseem a lot so she wanted to know where he failed because she didn't want to make the same mistake that contributed to his downfall.

"You're right..." Destiny replied then dropped her head to think fast. She popped back up and was ready to take them on. "Naseem was considering making a deal with the CIA."

Several members shifted in their seats and it appeared that they were uncomfortable with the statement.

"Yes, the CIA..." Destiny said, with the intent for the letters of the government top agency to sink in to the minds of the group. "As I've told this group before, almost two years ago that I didn't want to be apart of nobody helping the government or any government agency for that matter... I meant that, and by Naseem even thinking about considering the offer made me sick to my stomach. I knew that I was getting out and moving on with my love."

"Do you have proof of this betrayal by Naseem?" Jah- Key asked. He was sitting next to Crystal. Jah-key had got his dreads cutoff and was wearing a black suit. He was looking and feeling every bit of the boss that he was.

"We have proof of this..." She stopped for a second.

Destiny didn't know if she wanted to reveal this part but decided that it was a must. "I was with Naseem in Hong Kong when he was approached by an asset of the CIA... I heard with my own ears what they were purposing to Naseem. And, it was power! Power to control the whole US market... This deal was going to be bigger than money. The CIA was trying to make him KING, literally... Well, the man left the room then I stepped out from hiding. Naseem admitted to me that he wanted to consider the deal... Greed was seeping through his words and demeanor."

"Did you see what this man or woman looked like." Crystal asked.

"No, but I did see a picture of him later by another person who was also approached...

"I thought that family, integrity, honesty and never forgetting where we came from and who we were, were the principles and fabric of this group... A think that is what one of you said, in one of the meetings."

"Yes it was." Tony Rome said.

"Well, that is the principles that I stood on when Naseem considered this tragic choice... I let it be known to the powers that be and I've been rewarded by a having a direct line to the source of our business." Destiny stopped. She had to gain her thoughts.

"What was the purpose of this grand scheme that was thought up by several of you in attendance? Independence, and the ability to reign supreme in this business and distance ourselves from any foreign authority who also wanted to call the shots in our own backyards.

"We have the blue print for all of these goals." Destiny said and pointed to the folder. "We just got to stay the course and not let politics, envy, greed or favoritism divide us..."

"I agree with you but how do we know that what you say is true... Are we simply to take your word at face value? If, that's the case than any one of us come say that so-and-so is working with the authorities and that they should be dealt with..."

"You're absolutely right, Crystal... And, if you want or anybody in here wants too, I could present Naseem to you at the next meeting and have him explain the situation...

"Look, I was dragged in to the picture and luckily for everybody here, I was in that hotel room with Naseem... Now, Naseem wasn't going to let anybody know about this meeting so he could've mislead this whole group down the wrong road."

"You say, you see this person later... The so-called CIA agent."

"No, he's not an agent. He's an asset that is controlled and has close ties with the Colombians."

"Where are we at with him? He's still a potential threat... As, I understood from you on a prior occasion, he was trying to work both sides." Tony Rome said.

"Yes, he's still a threat to us. He could tip off the DEA or any other agency about our movements and shipments... But, the Matta family is dealing with this... It's out of..." Destiny said before reaching for the buzzing phone on the table. She grabbed it and seen that it was from Bonita.

The message line read 'urgent'. Destiny stated, "May you please excuse me but I have to view this video email."

Destiny scrolled through the video email then hit the play button.

Sebastian sat on his knees in the grass. He was naked, hunched over, with his hands tied behind his back. Two masked men wearing all black and bullet proof vests that had 'FARC' written in yellow on them were standing on both sides of Sebastian.

"Who are you?" A person said but could not be seen.

"Sebastian Gonzalez."

"Who do you work for?"

"I work for the CIA but I'm an international drug dealer who's wanted by many governments and I've killed many in order to get to the top."

"What do you deserve for your betrayal of the Central American people?"

"I deserve death for all of the atrocities that I done and ordered against my fellow Spanish speaking people."

A masked man came from the side of the camera and placed a rusty 9 millimeter to Sebastian's head and pulled the trigger. The bullet struck Sebastian on the left side of his temple. Upon impact of the bullet, blood gushed a few inches as Sebastian leaned to the right side then fell in the grass.

Destiny stopped the video then glanced around the room.

She didn't show any fear or shock from witnessing the murder of Sebastian. It was more like a relief for her. Now, she didn't have to worry about the CIA or Sebastian tracking her down.

She placed the phone on the table and smiled. "Well, we don't have to worry about Sebastian anymore... It seems like the Colombians have already fulfilled their part for us."

"What do you mean by that? Is he dead?"

"Yes, if this video is authentic, and I have no reason to doubt that it's not." Destiny said then passed the phone to her right.

The phone went around the table so that it could be viewed by all. Some showed disgust by the barbaric killing of a human being. These were the ones who didn't enjoy the fact of killing being involved with the selling of drugs. They were the ones who wanted it to be a non-violent business but it wasn't at times. And, violence was called on and metted out to balance the playing field of this business.

But at the end of the day, everybody appreciated the fact that Sebastian would be out of their hair. They wanted the government out of their business, and with Sebastian dead that's what they got; a stress free opportunity to make a bunch of money.

The phone made it back to Destiny. "Now, we're all on the same page... The Sebastian problem is fixed, and I'll present my evidence of Naseem's betrayal at the next meeting so that this international affair we have with the Matta family can move forward and make us all filthy rich."

"I agree..." Crystal said then the rest of the members started muttering the same thing.

Destiny had done it. She had convinced them that she could get things done and lead the people in the right direction by making the right choices. Now, Destiny only problem was with Naseem. He was still around, and a possible threat to her group and life. Destiny had learned a while back what desperation breeded and what some people were capable of doing under pressure. She needed this problem fixed. But, Bonita was in her way and protecting the potential Judas.

Everybody started filling out of the room. They headed for the exit. The group was trying to hurry and get back to their other responsibilities in life. Destiny sat there viewing the phone. "Damn, this woman has that much power!" She stated out loud to herself.

Destiny was excited that Sebastian met the destiny that he deserved. He had killed plenty of people for position, drugs, governments, and for other less than honorable reasons. The only concern she felt about the murder was that it was on tape, and he was CIA. She didn't mention it to the group but this incident could jeopardize their existence.

While viewing the video, at the table with the group, Destiny ran down the potential fallout for the killing. The CIA would want revenge on the killers. They would play hard ball and try to increase security around the ports of America. It would be a major investigation into the FARC and who paid them to kill a CIA asset. All of this ran through Destiny's mind, as each person viewed the phone.

After much back-and-forth with herself, Destiny started thinking of ways to exit this whole ordeal. It wasn't for her, she thought. The ideal of running a major importation ring, and distribution network throughout America was harder than most could think. You had to have eyes and ears everywhere in order to realistically protect yourself from any dangers.

Destiny closed her eyes and titled her head back a bit to rest on the fluffy chair. She couldn't believe that at the age of 35 years old that she had accomplished so much in such a short life span. "I came a long way from the slums of Miami." She thought to herself. Destiny had literally become the definition of a self-made millionaire. She had conquered the modeling world then went on to receiving the leading role of running an illegal Fortune 500 company that specialized in the product of cocaine. She was at the top of her game but Destiny didn't want it. But, Destiny had to fulfill her promise.

After Bonita confronted Destiny in New York about Naseem then showing her the pictures in Hong Kong the two had became close friends. Destiny flew regularly to Panama in order to discuss business and other important matters that were going on in America. And, it was during one of these visits that the two struck a deal.

Bonita had promised to take care of Sebastian and making sure to restore Destiny's public image. And, Bonita did just that. All, Bonita wanted in return was for Destiny to run the group, stay away from

Naseem, and maintain that the Matta family product was being sold on the America streets. Destiny upheld her part of the bargain but was still skeptical about a few things that constantly bothered her.

Destiny got up from the table then gathered her things. She had a few other important matters that she had to take care. And, one of those matters was the upcoming release of Polo.

Chapter 16

1 year later

"This nigga draw'in..." Polo said, to no one in particular. He was just speaking out loud, as he strutted out of the federal prison.

Polo turned around and took a last look at the prison he just finished a five year sentence in. It was the entrance to the medium-security level prison. Victorville Federal Correctional Institution splashed across the front of the building.

He shook his head then turned back around. Polo's past was behind him and all that laid ahead was his future. What, he was going to do with it was the question. But, Polo stared at the future right before his eyes.

A black Lamborghini, with yellow trimming around the edges and curves of the vehicle, was doubled park in front of the prison. The passenger side tinted window rolled down.

"Yo, it's me," was all that the driver said then rolled the window back up.

Polo smiled to himself. He seen the whole drama playing out. Polo had that type of hustler's intuition. The ability to foresee things happen before they actually do. And, with this little stunt right here, Polo knew exactly what the play was all about. Polo decided to play along with the game. After all, he would benefit from it anyway.

He headed to the expensive machine then stopped before grabbing the handle. Polo stared in to the tinted vehicle and couldn't see nothing but his reflection. He appeared the same from the view. In his early forty's his appearance didn't dramatically change since his arrest. The only thing that had changed was the cheap clothes that he wore, at the moment. Polo had left prison in a gray sweat suit and tan Timberland boots.

Polo grabbed the handle to let himself in. The suicide door lifted up then went to the front. Polo climbed inside the vehicle and closed the door.

The inside was immaculate. Black soft-leather seats with yellow trimming, and the word Centenario etched in yellow going across the passenger side dash.

"What's up bru? I'm glad you accepted this." Naseem said while extending his hand to Polo.

"Why wouldn't I... I love playing with the winning team." He said, before accepting Naseem's hands.

"I got everything set up for you... I know you're a man who is used to nothing but the best, so I made sure I laid everything out for you... I'm going to show you around the town and get you acquainted with the city and so we could talk."

"I'm pretty familiar with LA, and the Valley. I use to come out here pretty often with my buls."

"Oh okay, but a lot of things changed within the last five years so you might want to be reacquainted with a few things."

"That's cool with me." Polo didn't want to debate with the man. Especially with their relationship being fairly knew.

After Destiny spilled the news that Naseem was in contact with Sebastian, everything collapsed for Naseem. Bonita had approached him with the news and demanded that he explain himself to her. Bonita needed an answer; a legit reason why Naseem would collaborate with the same person who was responsible for her family's deaths. She couldn't understand how Naseem would do such a thing.

Naseem articulated the reasons properly. He had too. Naseem knew that it might've ended with a death sentence for him, if he didn't convince Bonita that he wasn't going take the deal. Naseem had explained that he was just buying time,in order to find a way to squash the threat. Bonita went for it. But, this was only because she loved him. Naseem had captured her love, and Bonita couldn't get around that fact. So, she went against all the rules of the underworld. Bonita didn't murder Naseem for the betrayal.

With the love and emotions pushed to the side, Bonita was a shrewd business woman though. She made Naseem relinquish his position in the group. He could only run the family businesses and the ones he had established on his own. With Naseem leaving the drug business alone, he would still have full access to everything that they built together. In the terms of spending the money and the living the high-life. But, Bonita made sure that Destiny was not to be seen or touched.

Bonita's jealousy of Destiny's affair with Naseem made her keep Naseem around her all the time. If she left the country on business, Bonita wanted Naseem to join her. And, it was the same if he had to leave the country. She was needy and insecure when it came to Naseem.

Naseem agreed to this arrangement. For the simple reason that, he actually loved Bonita and wanted her to be his wife. But, that didn't stop the fact that he wanted revenge. Naseem wanted to get even with Destiny. She had ruined his life, and tried to get him murdered.

"Ae bru, I won't be needing any place to stay either... I got a little young jawn out here that I'm going to be getting wit, so I'm good..." He said, without staring at Naseem.

"It's cool... I'm here if you need me. I got access to a lot of things out here... Everything, my nigga!"

Naseem's last words caught Polo off guard. "Everything like what? Coke and all that?"

"I got access to whatever you want."

"I'm definitely going to need that... We'll discuss that in a little bit. I got to touch bases with a few people back in Philly, and take care of this other little problem that I got... I got to reclaim the throne, and all of my riches that've been stolen by the bitch of mine."

"So, we're still on board with the Destiny project?" Naseem asked. He was desperate to get Destiny out of the picture even if it was working with a known rat. Naseem didn't care. He planned on taking care of the loose ends when she was dealt with.

"Oh course, you know more about her than me right now... The bitch stole everything from me, and I want every dime of it back... And, I'll die trying to get it... I'm not going to let that bitch spend it up, and strut around like shit sweet."

Naseem just nodded his head, and laughed to himself because he was the one who planted the seed in Destiny's head to take the money and assets.

"Whenever you're ready I'll set it in motion." Naseem stated trying to get a response from Polo. But, Polo sensed the deceit in Naseem's tone and demeanor.

"It'll be soon... Best believe that! It'll be soon... I just got to contact a few people that I haven't heard from in years then it's a go." Polo replied without giving Naseem any eye contact.

Polo had been in this predicament before. Murder was a deadly game to be played, and he had played with death on every level that a person could think of. So, he couldn't just go at Destiny without a plan. A plan to first get his money, kill Destiny then get rid of Naseem somehow. But, Polo needed time to figure this all out.

"I did want to ask you a question?"

"Go ahead."

"Do you know Alex Diaz?"

"Nah, but I can get some info on him... Why?"

"I just wanted to make sure you didn't fuck with him because he played a role in my little brother getting killed over some money."

Naseem glanced at Polo. He wanted to make sure that he remembered the face expression, tone of voice, and other characteristic that Polo displayed when lying.

Naseem knew the story well. Polo's brother Chance had been murdered in a home invasion because of his brother's reputations of being snitches, and that Chance was a young money getter.

Destiny had laid out the whole drama to Naseem. He knew about Alex Diaz, and how the drug lord told on Polo and Priest, in order to escape a huge federal sentence and about how the group owned an online gambling company worth billions now.

"I'll look around and see if I could come up with anything on this dude... Alex Diaz, you said his name was? Where's he from, and what cartel he ran?"

"Sinaloa Cartel!"

"I know who you're talkin about... He got ran out of Mexico for being a snitch... I think he told on his partner named Manny or something back in the day. Well, people found out and there was a price on his head for that... I heard he ran up there to Washington State. I'll get all the information on him."

"Please, I need it... He got to be held accountable for my brother's death."

Naseem didn't say a word. He concentrated on moving through the morning traffic of Interstate 15. He still couldn't believe how Polo was a piece of shit. Naseem hated snitches but he had to deal with it for the time being. Polo was the key to getting even with Destiny.

Naseem figured that since Polo was home and that Bonita already knew that Destiny stole his money, if Destiny was murdered that he could place the blame on Polo. All of the suspicion would be off of him and Polo would be the one who Bonita would think did it.

They rode in silence for a while. Polo was wrapped in his own thoughts. Five years of prison had took a little bit out of him. And, finally reality was smacking him in the face.

Polo was getting out of prison without any realistic plan. The whole time in, all he thought about was murdering Destiny, the lawyers and a few other people who contributed to his downfall. He didn't think about or come up with any legitimate, ideals to prosper in life once home. Now free, this disturbed Polo a little bit because he had a friend who still believed in him. She was a woman from the past who knew Polo when he was king.

Chanel lived in Vegas, and was a constant visitor at Federal Correctional Institute Victorville. The two had morphed into a couple over the years and Polo promised Chanel that he would come home to her. And, Polo was going to live up to that promise.

Naseem thought Polo was staying in Cali but he was wrong. Polo didn't trust nobody. He wasn't going to let Naseem know where he was going to lay his head. So he made sure that Chanel didn't come around to pick him up.

Polo wanted to keep Chanel hidden from all the carnage that he was about to deliver, and the other dangers that lurked on the horizon.

"Ae, don't turn around but I think this black SUV a few cars behind is following us... It been back there since we pulled out of the prison."

"Does it look like the Feds?" Polo asked.

"Nah, the guy is black and by himself, it looked like."

Brucie navigated the Ford Expedition through traffic. He had been tailing Naseem since they left FCI Victorville. Brucie had been given specific orders from Destiny. She ordered him to call her as soon as

Polo exited the building. Brucie didn't do it. He waited for an opportunity. Brucie wanted to show his loyalty to Destiny and murder Polo before reporting to her. But, the opportunity had pasted so far and now he had to let her know that Polo was out.

He grabbed the phone off the passenger seat then started the text.

Brucie: he's out... what to do next?

Destiny: nothing!!! just follow him n don't get noticed.

Brucie: I can take care of this.

Destiny: no!!! just do what I said... it's an order...

Brucie didn't respond back. He knew Destiny wanted him dead but didn't want him to do it. Then a text came in from Destiny.

Destiny: who is he with?

Brucie didn't respond because he knew if he told her that Naseem had picked Polo up and they were in the car together that she really wouldn't let him do it. He smiled and threw the phone on the seat. Brucie tapped the Tech 9 that sat on his lap which had a silencer attached to it. He was ready to make his bones or enhance his position as some would call it. Brucie stepped on the gas to speed up. He was trying to catch up to the Lambo.

"Yo, the fucking Expo just sped up trying to pull on the side..." Naseem yelled out right before reaching under the seat to grab his gun.

"Hit the gas! Fuck the shoot-out on the highway." Polo said. He wasn't trying to go back to the joint. "Hold up! Hold up! I want to see who it is first."

Brucie rolled up on the passenger side of the Lambo. The tinted window came down, quickly. "Oh shit, oh shit! Pull off, pull off!" Polo yelled at Naseem.

Naseem leaned over to catch a glimpse. "Oh shit!" Was all that you heard before shots rang out from the SUV.

Chapter 17

Jay stood in front of the oversized window, butt-naked, with his arms folded across his chest. He had just put Destiny to sleep with some vicious thug fucking.

He gazed across the illuminated City of New York. People were out and about. All types of activities were unfolding beneath Jay's very eyes; clubbing, dating, killing, robbing, stealing and regular citizens who were working their graveyard shifts. A lot of these individuals were just enjoying life while others were plotting and planning for their immediate futures and ultimate survival in the story of life.

Jay was part of the latter bunch. He was thinking about the ultimate survival, his next power move, and the picture was becoming clearer by the minute. It had been bleak at first. Especially before he got that urgent request from Abdul Walid to go snatch Destiny out of the bando. Which then lead to her befriending him and next to her falling madly in love with him.

He had the upper hand now, so he thought. But one thing was for certain and that was he had his hands on the pulse of the game which gave him a great advantage over the competition.

Destiny was eating out of the plum of his hands. She was, slowly, giving him the power that he'd always been grinding for.

It wasn't a decision that she made without running it past him first.

Lady luck had finally landed at his feet which he then pulled up, and threw her in the bed and dominated her. But, as the old saying goes, with more money comes more problems. And, more problems by the day were popping up. So, he had to deal with the latest drama—Polo.

Bonita had called earlier with the news that Brucie shot the Lambo up trying to kill Naseem and Polo. Her and Destiny spoke, by cell and arranged a meeting for everybody to attend on Saturday at Bonita's.

Jay got word to Tate who rounded up the hitters and sent them to the West coast ahead of the meeting.

Destiny didn't think it was that serious to send the squad out. But, she didn't tell none of them this. She left those types of decisions up to her boys.

Major, Jay and Tate agreed that it was a must that some goons head out. They didn't know Bonita or the family. What the boys did know was how to survive on them gritty streets. And, when it came to that gun-play being involved in the situation they took that serious, and to another level than most.

Jay shook his head because he knew regardless of how the situation went with Bonita that Polo had to die. It was mandatory and it had to be done immediately. He knew that with Polo's loose mouth everything could crumble before his very eyes. Too much was at stake with this coward living and he wasn't about to let another government witness ruin his well-being again.

He couldn't wrap his head around the scenario. Bonita had explained that Naseem and Polo survived the hit but was furious about the attempt. Nobody had ever tried him like that, and he considered this an ultimate act of war. Naseem wanted blood and he wanted it now.

Naseem begged for Bonita to green-light Destiny. He thought that Destiny had crossed a line. A line she couldn't recover from, which was a huge misstep.

Bonita wouldn't have it. She wasn't going to give Naseem the nod to slump Destiny. Bonita wanted to hear her side of the story.

Naseem couldn't believe it. He never seen Bonita act this sort of way when it involved family. Before she wouldn't have hesitated to give the nod for violating the family.

Bonita had told Destiny to lay-low for the time being. She could control Naseem but not Polo. Polo wasn't under her authority nor did she want him to be.

Destiny snuck up behind Jay. She was wrapped in a white sheet.

Jay flinched a little. He had been caught up in thought on how he was going to kill Polo.

"What's wrong?" She asked.

"You know what's wrong! The bul has to be dealt wit."

"I know..." Destiny replied.

"Why would you send that clown, Brucie, to handle such a delicate situation?" He asked with a slight grit.

"How many times do I have to explain to you that I did not tell him to do anything... He was suppose to just follow Polo, and find out where he was going."

"Come on man, stop bull-shitting. Was it that or did you really want to know if another jawn was coming to pick him up?" He asked with a hint of jealousy in his tone.

Destiny was crushed by the accusation. She couldn't believe that Jay thought she still had feelings for Polo. "What? You tripping now!"

"Why you couldn't just wait? I told you, Tate told you, and Major told you to leave it alone and that we were going to handle it."

"I know... I know.... I'm sorry. I get hard-headed at times. I just wanted to help."

Jay just shook his head. Destiny opened the sheet and wrapped Jay in it with her.

"Come on, let's go back to bed and enjoy the final night in my home...

I'm, so sorry baby." She stated with a sincere but a tease like voice.

Jay couldn't resist. Destiny had a way of breaking down the hard interior of Jay.

He bent down and kissed her on the forehead before wrapping his arms around Destiny's body. She closed her eyes and enjoyed the moment.

She needed the moment because deep inside, she was fighting her demons. After Brucie missed the opportunity to kill Polo, she started rethinking that it might not be a good idea to murder Polo.

She wanted him dead, but she didn't want him dead. Destiny was confused and even thought about giving Polo a nice sum of money to get on with his life. To leave the States or something. But, she knew that option wouldn't work. Polo grew up in the streets of North Philly. He killed his way to the top of the food chain. It was no way that he was going to take a punk-ass payoff and let her keep the rest. Destiny knew Polo would rather die than let her off that easy.

Destiny opened her eyes and stared at Jay. "Boo... Please, deal with this. My life is on the line."

"I know... I know... Believe me, I know how serious this is, and how deep it could get." Jay replied then snatched open the sheet. He picked Destiny up and carried her back to the bedroom.

* * *

A light drizzle fell on the forest green Escalade as it cruised down 195. Tate was behind the wheel, and heading to Manhattan to go catch up with his brother. Everybody had planned to leave from JFK on the same flight, and this included a few of the Brothers young boys who were heading over with them. These wasn't the designated hitters. Tate had sent them ahead already but these were the young boys who dumped a lot of the coke on the streets. Original Highland Gardens get money buls.

Tyson was leant back in the cushioned leather seat. He was a Garden

Boy Savage to the heart. Born and raised in the Highland Gardens and he'd been through the struggles that came with being a Garden Boy. Tyson was a gangsta and battled tested. This was so even at the tender age of 29 yrs old.

A few years back while the Brothers were away in hell, Tyson had to represent and put his thing down. It was around the time that another indictment came down in the Highland Gardens. The Cutt-Off or Circle of Death, as the Feds dubbed them, was another money getting area in the Gardens. Twenty-one people was arrested and charged in 81 count indictment. The Feds also confiscated 2 million dollars worth of drug money during their round ups. The 81 charges were part of the usual scheme of things. Drugs and guns were the topic.

With the Cutt-Off boys getting knocked, the next in line to fill that void was none other than Tyson. But instead of the usual drug of the Garden's; cocaine, Tyson decided to switch up and flood the streets with Loud.

Tyson had been introduced to A-Town from Oakland. The Oakland native had been in Chester laying low, on the run for a body, with a Thot who he had met during the All-Star game in LA. The Thot had been talking and spreading the word around Chester that A-Town had it. A-Town heard about the notorious Highland Gardens and how it would be a great spot to start a weed set. A-Town got the Thot to reach out to Tyson. The two got together and started doing business. But, A-Town started playing himself, and did the unthinkable. A-Town would front Tyson 50-to-60 pounds a week and triple the price on him. It was crazy and didn't make sense. Especially since A-Town had been relying heavily on Tyson for help. But the weed game was new terrain for Tyson, and he wanted to know the ins and outs of the business.

A-Town had Tyson going out to Northern California and dealing directly with the connect. He would then get the team, load the vans up, and have a few girls drive them back to Chester. It was to the point where Tyson had close to four-to-five hundred pounds of Loud under his control, and he never thought about crossing A-Town. Not until A-Town started driving the prices up when he knew how much the pounds were going for, and the other thing was that he tried to set him up.

A-Town had caught a gun case. He was driving on his way to the casino and task force pulled him over. The drug task force found a gun and asked A-Town to cooperate on the spot or else he was going to jail. He jumped at the opportunity. Especially since they didn't know who he was. A wanted murderer.

Word got around the City that A-Town had got gripped with a gun, and didn't go to jail. A-Town didn't hear the rumor nor did the little Thot that he was in love with. But Tyson did hear it.

He investigated the matter and was convinced that it was true.

Tyson set the plan in motion. He called A-Town around to the trap. Tyson had told him that a person was interested in grabbing a hundred pounds for an unreasonably high price. A-Town's greed made him go against his first rule of moving around in the day time and serving Chester niggas himself. Tyson needed him to come out during the day because the Thot would be at work, and he could get his young bul App to run up in the house and take all the money and Loud.

A-Town came around to the trap spot on McCarey Street but he just rode past the house. He would, usually, circle the block a few times before stopping to go into the house. It was a little pattern that he had, and Tyson knew this. So when A-Town spun the corner a few times he went and stopped in front of Demarco's and called Tyson to make sure everything was cool. He didn't have the pounds on him but they were at the house. A-Town had planned on having Tyson transport them back to the Gardens. But Tyson had a different plan. He ran from behind the dumpster then torn A-Town apart.

The hit had been legendary. After A-Town was murdered, rumors shot through the city that Tyson had killed A-Town and hit a lick for a half-of-million. Tyson wouldn't confirm it or deny it. He loved to keep the niggas guessing. But, in truth, all he got was the 50 pounds after the split with App. A-Town had cleared the house and sent all of his money back to Oakland when he had decided to be a snitch.

Tate glanced at Tyson a few times but continued to talk on the cellphone. "Yo, Dre said what up?"

"Let him know I said wass up, my nigga."

Tate shook his head then said a few more things to Dre on the phone. He then passed the phone to Tyson. "Its Nier G's on the phone."

Nier and Dre were cellys. They were doing time in the United States Penitentiary in West Virginia—Hazelton. It was a violent prison.

The two had just been released from the Special Housing Unit and were trying to get back to chasing a dollar on the penitentiary yard.

They had been placed in the SHU due to a stabbing that the prison officials couldn't prove they did because it happened in a cell. Out of view of the prison surveillance system, and the prison's human cameras.

During their hole time, the two ran into B, a snitch from Dre's case. They planned day and night on how to catch him in the recreation yard but it never happened. The staff at USP Hazelton had, immediately, caught the mistake of the snitch being there, and shipped him two days later. But just knowing that he was on the tier and in the same prison as them, led them to a venting session.

They went back and forth about how prison and Chester had changed. You couldn't be a snitch, rat or cooperating witness in the USP's. More importantly, in Chester during the mid-nineties and early 2000's you, definitely, couldn't be a snitch. The niggas and bitches wouldn't mess with you. You'd be an outcast. It was different now. Social media had changed everything and gave these chumps a platform to boast about their snitching escapades. They were trying to make it seem cool and that all the other people who had morals were wrong for standing up. And, now they had started gaining a following with these women who were embracing these suckers and still giving them the pussy. It was insane but this was the reality.

Tyson grabbed the cell with a huge smile. The two had grown up together in the Gardens, and played by some of the same rules.

Nier G's had been grabbed by the Feds and thrown on the Cutt-Off indictment. At the time, he was the youngest person on the indictment but yet labeled the most ruthless. This label was attached to him by the Feds and the goons alike.

Nier gained this status or reputation by being a hitter on them streets. It was crazy because in reality, Nier was a hustler first and shooter second.

The Feds didn't see it that way though. They rounded up the cooperating witnesses, and promised all types of outrageous deals to tell.

It had been rumored that Nier was responsible for three bodies, personally, but it couldn't be proven in the court of law. Therefore, the Feds was only able to charge him with conspiring to sell five kilos or more of cocaine; basically, a federal drug charge that earned a mandatory ten year sentence. But when the smoke cleared, Nier received a 15 year sentence in the feds. He wasn't so lucky in the State though.

By the Feds failing to prove that certain murders were in furtherance of Nier's conspiracy to sell drug charge, they had to hand over the violent offenses to the State of Pennsylvania. Nier was charged with one murder, and two attempted murders. He took a deal and received a 16-40 year sentence which he didn't take to lightly.

Nier hated that he had to take the deal but he didn't want to roll the dice and crap out like the Boyle Street Boys had done and ended up with multiple life sentences.

He planned to make them niggas who told on him pay for taking his life and youth. And, the crazy remarks and pictures that Scooby, Bird,

Craig and Fat Dre put on Facebook had pushed him over the limit. Several of them had been boasting about Nier doing 40 years and how they were happy about it. This didn't sit well with him or Dre. They planned to make them niggas pay for disrespecting a real nigga, and the culture as a whole.

"Damn wass up, my nigga? I haven't heard from you in a minute... When you get up there wit Dre?" Tyson said then puffed on the Dutch.

"I been up here for like 6 months... Man, I had got caught up with some shit at the other spot. You know how that shit is..." Nier replied. He was laid back in the bunk with a grey sweatsuit on.

It was lockdown time. They had the lights out, and were just taking in the moment of talking to the brus.

"No doubt... Gotta get to that bag."

"Yeah, but you see what them niggas saying and posting on Facebook?"

"I read that shit... You know they social media gangstas now... Believe me, they ain't coming up the way or showing up at any of the bars or parties... You already know niggas on they ass 'bout that shit they did to y'all."

"Yo, I need the bul number... Young bul Meer. He wit y'all now? I know he be moving with y'all now..."

"Nah, them niggas out right now but I got his handle for you... Why wass up? You need me to handle some shit." Tyson was confused by Nier asking for Meer number.

"Ya phone straight?"

"Yeah, it's a throw away."

"We just got this one too. It's clean for now... But, I need you to make Meer, and them lean on them rat ass niggas... Look man, kill all them

165

rat ass Cutt-Off niggas... Start getting them niggas plucked... One by one, so I can sleep better at night. Then start hitting them other hott-ass niggas who told on Dre and them."

"Yo'll, shit kinda different right now... We getting to a bag right... A bag on whole 'nother level, bru... That might draw on us but I'll see what I can do."

"Yo, come on bul... We go back to far for that... Tyson make that shit happen, my nigga... Them niggas don't deserve to be breathing the same air as real niggas... You feel me! Do this favor for me... Matter of fact, not just for me but for the culture. We need to get this shit back in order. Everything is fucked up now 'bout the game."

"What Dre say 'bout this?" Tyson asked the question because he knew Dre was trying to make a play for the streets. He had several appeals in the courts, and a federal witness getting murdered from his case would surely cause problems with Dre's chance of freedom.

"He on board..."

"I'm going to see man..."

"Yo'll, I'm going to get at y'all tomorrow. Don't forget 'bout me bru."

"Yo already know that real niggas do real things... I'm on it, bru." Tyson said before hanging up.

Tate glanced over at Tyson. He had been listening to the conversation but didn't hear what Nier was saying. "Everything good?"

"Yeah, Nier just in there stressing a little bit... He good though... I got him..." Tyson replied before hitting the Dutch.

Tate didn't respond but felt that something was wrong with Tyson. He didn't want to push the issue though. He trusted Tyson and accepted his word as the truth. Tate didn't have no reason not to.

Chapter 18

Bonita reclined back on the leather sofa. This was her usual spot. She loved it. The spacious living room provided her with a unique feeling of comfort. Especially when she had the two oak doors opened to the yard. Maybe it was the solitude of Malibu's high hills and mountains or the scenic view that her home came with or maybe it was just the fact that this room provided her with a space to think without all of the world's many distractions.

Paris stepped out of the kitchen and headed over to the living room. She was dressed in business attire with a pair of black heels, a black skirt and white blouse. She carried an iPad in one hand, and a cup of green tea in the other. She reached Bonita and tried to hand her the cup.

"Thank you, Paris but you can sit it on the table..."

Paris sat the cup down then stepped over to the sofa across from Bonita. She placed the iPad on the table then sat back, crossed her legs, and stared at Bonita. "Well, how are you going to handle this situation? I wanted to know because you have yet to explain to me on how you were going to deal with Destiny."

Bonita never took her eyes off of the manicured lawn. She was in deep thought but yet still undecided with the issue. It was true that she owed Naseem her loyalty but Destiny was the future.

She had big plans for Destiny, and the group. Bonita didn't want the cornered market, that Destiny held control of, to slip out of the Matta's family grip.

"What do you think I should do? I'm sorry that I haven't asked for your advice on this. But I'm still undecided... I don't know whether to punish her or not." Bonita replied taking her gaze off of the lawn for the first time.

"We have to hear her side of the story first. Second, why was Naseem even with this man, Polo . I mean, everybody knows that he testified against his brother... Are we going to get an answer on that topic?"

"Yes! Naseem is upstairs getting dressed. I thought about asking him first before Destiny arrived."

"That would be a good idea. I don't understand why this wasn't explained to you already... I mean..."

"I didn't want to hear it." Bonita said, cutting off Paris in mid-sentence.

"So how can you sanction or punish Destiny? I'm pretty sure she wants Polo dead for a number of reasons. And, I'm pretty sure she didn't expect Naseem to be in the car with him."

Bonita shook her head in agreement with what Paris had said. It was true and Destiny had already explained the problem to Bonita. "I understand..." Was all that she could muster before seeing Hector running towards her from the yard.

Before Hector reached the doors, a loud humming noise could be heard coming from the backyard.

Paris leaped up off of the sofa. "What the hell is that?" She said, a little alarmed.

Bonita just stood there. She never got up nor made a move.

"It sounds like a helicopter passing through the sky but it sounds very close."

"To damn close, if you ask me... Are you expecting somebody to arrive this way?"

"No..."

The humming sound of the chopper was getting closer and seemed like it was right above Bonita's home.

Hector made it to the doors. He had an assault rifle clutched in his hands, and he appeared alarmed by the noise. Hector tried to close the huge doors but was stopped by Bonita.

Miguel stormed through the hallway that lead to the living room. He was followed by six men wearing dark glasses, black suits and carrying assault rifles.

The presence of Miguel running towards the room startled Bonita. She got up when Miguel entered the room.

"Ms. Matta, we have trouble."

"What! Who?" Bonita asked a bit concerned.

"I don't know who this is but there's two helicopters above the house, and one is circling the home."

Bonita turned then stared out towards Hector. He had five other men with him. They had their guns raised high and ready to shoot the choppers down.

"Come on! We need to get you, two, to the safe spot." Paris started to follow Miguel's orders. She was scared and didn't understand what was going on.

Bonita headed in Miguel's direction but stopped upon hearing the announcement coming from outside.

"Don't shoot! Don't shoot! This is Agent Michael Green with the CIA. We're here to talk." Agent Green screamed through the bullhorn. "Place your guns down or we will shoot... We're here just to talk." He repeated.

Two of the helicopters had men hanging out of the sides. They had .50 caliber machine guns trained on Hector and his crew.

"Tell them to lower their guns! Now!" Bonita yelled at Miguel. "Now!" She repeated when he gave her that unsure stare.

Miguel relayed the message to Hector. He responded and ordered his men to lower their weapons but not place them on the ground.

Agent Green seen that they lowered the weapons then ordered for his helicopter to land. The pilot landed on the lawn. The two other helicopters kept their guns trained on Hector's crew.

Agent Green leaped out of the chopper. He wore a black business suit with black tennis shoes that resembled boots. He was followed by three gun toting men who wore Swat like outfits with their faces covered. They headed towards the living room doors but before he got close enough Agent Green waved his hand across the throat. The pilot shut the engine off, and the two other helicopters spun off to patrol the surrounding area.

Bonita walked towards the yard. She motioned for Hector to stand down and let the Agent in the house.

Agent Green approached the doors then stepped in. The three gun totters followed suit and entered behind him.

"Why the grand entrance?" She asked a bit surprised by Agent Green arrival in Malibu.

"I was hoping to try those new 50's out that we got." He replied in a serious tone.

Bonita waved him over to the sofa. He declined the offer. Agent Green stood in the middle of the room and Bonita stood right in front of him.

The three masked men spread out across the room and trained their eyes on Hector and his crew. Their guns were lowered but fingers remained on the triggers.

The atmosphere was tense. Paris stepped up next to Bonita. She wanted to help her friend and sister remain strong during this strained encounter.

"What can I do for you than Agent Green?"

"Were you involved with the murder of Sebastian? He was one of mine!" Agent Green asked with a commanding tone.

"No." Bonita said, with a convincing demeanor.

The room remained still. Bonita's last words depended on the outcome of this encounter.

After Sebastian was murdered, the killing appeared on the internet and spread across the intelligence community like wild fire. The CIA stepped in to investigate the murder and concluded that it was done by the Colombian drug lord Diego Perez-Henao.

What they couldn't agree on was whether the Matta's had any connection to it. So, in order to clear up the suspicions, Agent Green wanted to meet and see firsthand whether Bonita was connected to Sebastian's murder.

Agent Green sized Bonita up, quickly. She convinced him of her innocence but his experience with these type of criminals made him think otherwise.

"Ms. Matta, I came here looking for answers but I still haven't received them... Before Sebastian was murdered, he made you an offer. That is null and void. The agreement between us that had been understood with your family, as before, remains in effect... That is until further notice. And, I say further because I want to make sure that you didn't have anything to do with the killing of a CIA agent..."

"I can assure you that nobody in my family had anything to do with Sebastian's death."

"But, we will bring Diego to justice... So don't get to comfortable with doing business with him." Agent Green said then turned around and headed for the doors.

The three masked men secured Agent Green's departure before following him to the helicopter.

The helicopter lifted in the air then took off through the hills. The other choppers followed closely behind until they disappeared in the horizon.

Naseem ran down the steps carrying an assault rifle. He reached Bonita who was sitting next to Paris on the sofa.

"Are you okay?" He asked.

"Yes, now go put that thing up before the guest arrive."

"What happened? Nobody came and told me anything." Naseem said while staring around at all the security guys.

They had failed to alert Naseem on what was transpiring in the house.

"It happened so quick... Nobody had enough time to alert any one." Bonita said.

"Well, what happened?"

"Just some people asking about Sebastian. I'll explain later, honey."

Naseem was seething. He stormed off then headed back upstairs to his room.

Bonita ordered everybody back to work. She was upset at them, and planned on firing the whole crew. They had just committed a very serious breach of security letting those agents slide up on her home like that. Bonita planned to address the issue later because she couldn't at the moment. She still had to entertain Destiny.

A few hours went past. Bonita and Paris discussed other important business matters at length. They were deep in to a topic when Hector stepped into the room.

"Ms. Matta, your guest have just arrived. They're waiting in the front."

"Bring them in please."

Destiny strutted through the hallway flanked by Major, Jay and Tate. The group was all business, and ready for any unexpected surprises by the Matta's.

Destiny stepped into the room first. She was dressed in a tan skirt, white blouse and wore a black jacket over the top with black heels. Destiny's hair was pulled back in a bun and she wore some light make-up on her face.

Bonita headed over to greet Destiny. The two met with a hug and kiss on the cheeks. It was all love between the two. Bonita didn't bother to address the men.

She waved Destiny over to the sofa where Paris sat. Destiny accepted the invitation and sat down next to Paris. Bonita walked over to the other sofa then sat down.

Major and the Brothers stood behind the sofa. They were strapped up and thugging to the fullest. All of them had regular street gear on. Blue jeans, tan Timbs and T-shirts. Destiny had informed them not to dress up. She wanted Bonita to think that they were just regular niggas. Destiny didn't want to expose her hands to Bonita, and let her see who she had running her empire.

Naseem came down the steps. He had changed into a tailored- made, grey, business suit. He wore a white shirt, and dark blue tie with it. Naseem went over and sat next to Bonita.

Bonita glanced at Naseem then addressed Destiny. "Now, I'm going to get straight to the point... Why were you trying to kill my fiance? I thought we agreed on this point?"

"With all due respect Bonita, I didn't try to kill Naseem... I had, specifically, ordered Brucie not to shoot."

"How do we know that's the truth?" Naseem asked in an aggressive tone.

Jay tensed up at the outburst. He didn't like the squeaky clean Naseem.

173

At least, not the Naseem that acted as if he didn't come from the slums. Jay knew him, and Titan. They were both products of Chester.

Bonita placed her hand on Naseem's leg. She didn't want him to speak, at the moment. This point had already been discussed by them and he was already violating the terms.

Destiny reached back to Tate. He handed her a phone. She scanned through it then found what she was searching for.

"Here... Here's the proof... I told Brucie not to do it."

She handed the phone to Bonita.

Bonita reviewed the text. She then handed it to Naseem, in order for him to view.

"Okay now, I want to know why was Polo in that vehicle with you?" asked Destiny.

A buzzing sound went off. A text had just come through on Tate's phone. He snatched the phone out of his pocket then viewed it.

Meer: ol' head, we can't find a low spot

Tate: go head n fall back... we good!

He replied to the text.

"It's a long story." Was all he could muster up without looking at Destiny.

"We have time, so go ahead and please inform us of why you had this federal informant in the car with you." Bonita asked in a sincere but authoritative voice. She wanted to know also. It was a mystery to her.

Naseem glanced at Bonita. He couldn't believe that she put him on Front Street, and was going against him in front of the people.

"I'll explain to you later... She doesn't need an excuse of why I do things..."

"I'm afraid I do, Naseem... If, I had to come out here and explain myself to you and Bonita, I think I deserve the same."

"She's right Naseem... I don't want her to jump to conclusions or me for that matter."

"Exactly because he knows what Polo has put me through... I don't have to justify my reasons for anything that I want done to him."

Naseem didn't bother to answer Destiny. He couldn't even stand looking at her no more. Naseem wanted her dead and planned on achieving that soon.

Jay leaned over then whispered in to Destiny's ear. "Go ahead and give the pussy a way out... Don't press him to answer the question."

Destiny nodded and accepted his advice. She then turned to Bonita. "So, is this problem solved? I didn't order the shooting nor do I want any problems with Naseem."

"Yes, I accept your truth... But, we have to deal with this Polo, guy. He could be big problems for us."

"I understand and I'll deal with it."

Bonita stared at Naseem. She wanted him to make peace with Destiny. He got the stare and dreaded his response. "I'll stay out of your business. I'm going to leave it alone, and I understand that those bullets weren't meant for me." Naseem said.

Destiny didn't believe his words. They weren't sincere to her. She did have a little bit of street smarts, and those instincts were telling her that Naseem was going to be her next problem.

After Naseem spoke, he stood up to shake Destiny's hand.

She accepted the apology, for the moment.

Bonita followed suit, and stood up along with Paris. Everybody exchanged shakes and hugs before concluding the meeting.

Everybody started leaving the room. Bonita stopped Destiny, as the others kept on heading towards the foyer.

She whispered in Destiny's ear. "I know where Polo is hiding at right now... I'll give you the address, if you promise to let me deal with Naseem, in order to clear this matter up."

Destiny was startled. She couldn't believe that Bonita seen through her whole fake performance. But, she kept it up. Destiny screwed her face up, and acted confused by the request. "What are you talking about? I'm done with the issue. So please give me the info."

Bonita just smiled then nodded to Paris who was standing by the front door. Paris handed Destiny a piece of paper. She took it then stepped out of the door.

Destiny turned back and glanced at Bonita. She motioned with her lips, thank you, but nothing came out. Bonita understood the gesture and hoped Destiny took care of the problem so she didn't have to.

Chapter 19

Destiny and the boys flew back east. They had planned to get back to business, and continue getting money. All of the drama, and underhanded moves by Naseem was coming to an end. Destiny had vowed to the boys that, if Naseem got in their way again he would definitely be sleeping with Biggie Smalls. They agreed too.

Major understood her worries but he had his own. Polo was out of prison, and they had a location on him. So time was of the essence.

Before flying out, Tate had the young hitters go out to Vegas and investigate the terrain. They wanted to make sure that he was out there. Who he lived with? And other things of that nature. Polo wasn't the average hustler. Destiny didn't know if he still had ties with any other major players so they had to come correct and be careful. It wasn't just her; everybody wanted him dead and the hit to go smoothly. They couldn't take any chances, this could be the last time that they could get a line on him before he gained any power.

* * *

The huge S550 Benz was double-parked in front of DeMarco's. Tyson sat in it under tint. He was on the phone with Muscle who had just closed a deal with Nordstrom's in order to place Garden Boy Savage clothing line on the selves. Nordstrom's had promised to place the line in about 100 stores nationwide. The GBS brand was about to take off, and the two childhood friends could vision the outcome, and all the legitimate money that they were about to make off of it.

Tyson closed the call with Muscle then reached in the astray to grab his Dutch. He fired it up and took a long pull on it. Tyson blew out the exotic smoke. The weed had did its duty, and brought immediate simulation to his brain. Tyson needed this relaxation. Things had been kinda hectic lately.

After hanging up with Nier the other day, Tyson thought long and hard about what Nier wanted him to do; killing federal witnesses. Not just any federal witnesses but witnesses who were still working with the Fed's. Ever since Dre and the Boyle Street Boys got convicted for killing a federal witness, niggas in the hood thought twice about it. Everybody knew that killing witnesses brought a whole different type of drama with it. But, this was Nier! Tyson said to himself on numerous occasions.

Tyson didn't run the request by the Brothers. And, he wasn't going to either. He knew what they would've suggested. They didn't want the heat. The Brothers were making more money than they had ever seen before. More money than a lot of niggas every seen before. And, they were doing it under the radar. So, he knew what the answer to that would be.

He had made the decision though. Tyson said, fuck it. He was going to do it for the culture. For the Gardens. But more importantly, he was going to do it for Nier. A real gangsta who deserved to be respected in the streets, in prison, and in death.

Tyson knew that, if the shoe was on the other foot that Nier would've done it for him without any second guessing. He was just that type of gangsta nigga.

Tyson reached in the seat to grab his phone and said, "Idris."

Idris picked up on the second ring. "Wass up, ol' head?"

"You around? I need a sit down wit you niggas... I got a job for y'all."

"Nah, we still out Vegas but we'll be back tomorrow night."

"Aight... Just in time for that 'Always on Point' show that we throwing for the youngbuls up top..."

"Oh yeah! Damn, I'm definitely trying to be up in that jawn."

"Get wit me when y'all get back aight."

"Aight."

"One." Tyson replied then hung up.

It was on. The deal had been sealed. Tyson had already run the lick past the young hitters. They knew how serious the mission was, and that it had to be done in secret. The Brothers couldn't know about the hits. They would go crazy, and try everything in their power to prevent such a crazy act. But, the youngsters wanted to do it. They had love for Nier too, and they wanted to pay homage to the ol' head hitter; one of the original goons of the Highland Gardens.

Tyson just shook his head. "Fuck it! They don't deserve to breathe a real nigga air." He said, while pulling off on to Highland Avenue.

Stay tuned…

Destiny

ABOUT THE AUTHOR

Andre 'Dre' Cooper is the author of *The Life We Chose 1 & 2, Betrayal of Sinners* and *Bullied*. He grew up in the poverty-stricken city of Chester. Where he saw the most vivid aspects of crime and violence being committed at the young age. He now writes about those experiences, not to glorify it, but to help others understand how it is coming up in America's forgotten slums. He has been imprisoned since 2003.

Andre 'Dre' Cooper is currently hard at work penning a memoir titled *"From Gangsta To Muslim, The Fed Story"*.

Andre "Dre" Cooper

Also by the author

The Life We Chose

The Life We Chose 2

Betrayal of Sinners

Bullied

All books and ebooks are available at Amazon.com.